WHO FOLLOWS

a gripping, dramatic, intense and suspenseful thriller

DIANE M DICKSON

Paperback published by The Book Folks

London, 2020

Mass market paperback (2)

ISBN 978-1-80462-305-3

www.thebookfolks.com

For my family.

PART ONE

Chapter 1

The first sighting was in Costa, the one by the market, not the one by the station. She was sitting at an outside table, smoking. Her long fingers flicked and twitched, knocking off the ash. I watched her drawing deep drags, not playing at the thing but really smoking. She was blowing smoke slightly off to one side so it didn't curl back into her eyes.

I don't approve of smoking, but watching her lips pursed around the cigarette and her eyelids pinching slightly as she inhaled, something touched me. I felt the attraction reaching deep inside to a place I thought was dead.

Her hair, blonde and a bit wispy, was caught up in a messy sort of knot on the top with something hard and plastic holding it together. Her fingernails were long and painted deep red. She seemed possessed of a magic field drawing me to her, separating her from the hoi polloi and gilding her with a glow of specialness. I watched for a little while from the back of the café but then she glanced at me a couple of times and I knew she had seen me, so I left.

After a few days I had consigned the occasion to memory – a ship passed and all that. Then I spotted her in Smiths. She was queuing at the till by the door with a magazine and I was able to slip in close behind her. She smelled good, perfumed but discreetly, something gentle and girly. I edged even nearer… meadows in the summer and apple orchards… my eyes closed as I inhaled the freshness of her.

I paid for my paper and scuttled out in time to follow and see where she went. She turned into the block beside the post office. I hung around, it was cold but I needed to know whether she worked there or was just visiting. After about three-quarters of an hour I surmised that she worked there. I crossed the pavement and examined the name plates on the door. It was one of those old Victorian buildings that had been a bank but was now taken over by several small businesses. Cho Lee imports, Taylor and Spry Investments and Hummingbird. There was nothing more, just Hummingbird. I had no idea what Hummingbird might be or do. *Strange.* Was she with Taylor and Spry? Cho Lee was probably Chinese but that meant little really. It wasn't based on any sort of logic but it appealed to me that this stranger would work for a company called Hummingbird, doing heaven knows what.

I had to leave then and get back home and down to work. There was a deadline looming on a site I was designing and so much else that was calling out for me. Sitting before my desk I knew I was going to do it before I did it. I had made the decision deep in my subconscious and wasn't the least bit surprised when my fingers, seemingly of their own volition, googled Hummingbird. Well, have you ever googled Hummingbird? There were more than fifteen million results. I couldn't do it then, there was no time. It would have to wait until I had the leisure to hone the search. In truth I needed to be calmer than I was with recent events fizzing in my mind.

The next day, visiting the mall again I felt myself searching just hoping on the off chance that I would see her, and there she was in Costa. It has been my experience that if someone works near a Costa and you see them in there twice at lunch time then it is one of their favourites. She bought a latte and some sort of pastry. She sat outside again with her cigarette. I didn't go in but I stood across the road; her movements fascinated me. She displayed such an unconscious grace and fluidity of movement. She was wearing a grey top and a multi-coloured skirt made from some sort of floaty material. It was moving with the breeze, catching at her long legs and flipping around her knees. She didn't fuss with it, just sat calm and at ease. I was mesmerized.

Chapter 2

I go down there most days now, down to the market to watch outside Costa. I have to be careful, of course, not to stand in the same place too often or look as though I am loitering with some suspicious intent.

It's easy if you pretend to look in the shop windows. Sometimes I go into the shops. Waterstones is a good one because you can stand near to the window and pretend to peruse the books. There's a little stationery shop as well that was quite useful. Yesterday, though, I had to buy a greeting card because one of the assistants became much too pushy. She tried to engage me in conversation about my choice. In the end I snatched up the nearest thing to hand. There was a stick man and woman on it dressed like a bride and groom and some idiotic nonsense scrawled inside. "Was I going to a wedding?" she wanted to know. Well that was the last time that I could use that shop, wasn't it, stupid girl. I was put completely out of sorts and as I left, I turned to find her tittering with her colleagues. I was infuriated but, in the end, it doesn't matter – as I say, there are plenty of little places to hover and wait and watch. She is usually on her own, I like that, no gangs of giggling women and no men, not even one.

I usually follow her back to the old building, Hummingbird. After that I go off home to have a drink and let my mind wander and imagine the day when I will sit with her at Costa. We will take our coffee together and chat about our plans for later. I see myself leaning over and stroking the errant strands of hair back from her face and maybe brushing a pastry crumb from the front of her dress. It will be done discretely but we will both smile at the little contact, reminded of our times together. I will go and meet her from work, of course, once we get together. I will walk down there each evening and we will either go and have a drink or maybe come straight home and make our evening meal. I wonder, will it be dinner or supper? She looks to me as though she will call it dinner, not tea though, oh no never that.

I am starting to think about colour schemes and so on now; I will have to redecorate this place when she comes here. I can tell from the way that she dresses that she is interested in colour. I am probably going to get some paint charts and fabric swatches in preparation. Best to be ready because I want her to understand that I will do whatever she wants to make her comfortable and happy.

Chapter 3

I have decided. Today is the day to make my move, it's now two months since the first sighting of my angel and the time has come. From first thing this morning my entire wardrobe has been thrown hither and thither across the bedroom, this first meeting must be perfect, so much is dependent on the way that it goes.

In the end my choice has been made. I don't want to appear too formal and overdone but do want to show right from the first instance of our real relationship that my standards are very high. Of course, Hummingbird – that is the name that I know her by and oh how it suits her – has very high standards of appearance herself. Mostly her clothes are feminine and pretty. Last Wednesday she was a vision in a pale green dress and cream shawl and it took all of my resolve and discipline not to declare myself there and then. I was rendered helpless by the sight of her. She seemed to me a woodland sprite, a nymph, something otherworldly and magical. The flimsy green stuff fluttered around her knees and the shawl caressed her arms, the fringes dancing in the small breeze as she sat at her favourite table.

The only small conundrum at the moment is exactly that – the favourite table. It is one of the outside ones that look over the pedestrianised area of the mall, near the big seats. Now, on the one hand it makes life so much easier at the moment, affording as it does so very many options for observation. However, the reason for her sitting there is of course the smoking. I admit to being fascinated by the movements and actions of her hands lighting the cigarette and carrying it to and from her mouth, the tiny bones moving and flexing under her fine skin, her slender fingers flicking and twitching. However, she will of course have to give up smoking as soon as we are together. One memorable day I did manage to slip into the table just behind her and it would have been absolute bliss if it hadn't been for the smoke blowing back into my face. Of course I know that she will be more than happy to forfeit this dubious pleasure for the sake of our relationship but it is something that must be understood from the very start.

Well, I have examined my appearance now from all angles and can declare myself satisfied. These trousers are new enough to be smart but old enough not to appear too contrived and my shirt is plain fine cotton which never lets one down, in my opinion.

Off we go now; a little early but I can't wait any longer. The butterflies in my stomach turn somersaults as I slam the door and pop the key under the rock beside the door. The windows are shining in the sun and the garden is neat and pretty. I have spent most of the last three days preparing the house just on the off chance that she will come back with me immediately, although I do understand that is rather unlikely.

Chapter 4

Oh, my goodness, I'm quite overcome, my hands are shaking and I have a quivering in my gut. In some strange way it is pleasant, a little like childish excitement on Christmas Eve. I need a stiff drink.

In truth the day did not go quite the way that I had planned. On leaving the house my intention was to make this the day that we actually met, the day that we started our lives together. It made sense to arrive early and thereby be in situ by the time Hummingbird arrived for her lunch.

I was horrified to find there was a nasty common family sitting at our table. By now I feel quite justified calling it our table. A horrible half-dressed woman with tattoos on her shoulder sat beside two really dreadful children. The children ate pastries and played with electronic games while their mother screeched into her mobile telephone. I was disturbed and perplexed and could do no more than wait across the street in Waterstones. Thankfully it wasn't long before the nasty creatures left and before there was a chance for any more invasions, I hurried across to Costa.

The mess was appalling. There were crumbs on the table, cups and plates lay about and grease and debris littered the chairs and the floor. Well, of course it was absolutely unthinkable that I should take the seat and I was certain that my angel wouldn't sit amongst that debris. What to do. After a moment's thought I took the plunge and seated myself at the square table adjacent to the favourite. It was possible, of course, that this could work to my advantage. Being the only other vacant place, it would be impossible for her to sit anywhere else. Oh yes, I thought, my very lucky day in the end.

I was beside myself with anticipation. I wasn't nervous, simply excited. The outcome was a foregone conclusion. I did want to make sure that the first meeting went well. To that end I mulled over the possibilities for my opening gambit.

As the time went on, I began to worry that maybe she wouldn't come at all but a few minutes later than usual I saw her rounding the corner. She headed for the disgusting mess that was her usual spot. My stomach was turning somersaults and I have to admit that my palms were damp, I was in such a fever of anticipation. Discretely I pushed the spare chair at my table a little outwards to make it easier for her to join me, a subliminal invitation if you will.

I freely admit that the next few moments plunged me into an agony of disappointment. She saw the detritus at her usual spot and I readied myself. Smiling in a friendly open way I waited for her to approach and make the request to join me. But no, imperiously she raised a hand and waved to the girl inside indicating the state of the table and chairs and then she stood aside as the mess was cleared away.

I was quite turned around by this development. My plans were now in some disarray as I was already seated and served. It was impossible that I should deliberately walk across to join her. It was vital that she had joined me, that's obvious, isn't it?

So in the face of what appeared to be a total disaster why should I now be so excited and overcome with passion? Well, she was wearing the green dress ensemble again with the gorgeous cream shawl. In order to reserve her seat, she draped the shawl over the back of the chair and then went to collect her coffee. She had never done that before; it was a day of surprise and change all around.

I had to be quick. The decision was instant as I acted without hesitation. I left my table and walked without pause past the seat. As I passed, I pulled the shawl to me and tucked it into my jacket. I have it now, here in my hand. The sensible part of me denies it but I am convinced that it is still warm from the touch of her skin. It smells of her, it is redolent of her beauty. I have it here now, against my cheek; the softness caressing my face as just a few short hours ago it caressed her arm. A prize, my treasure.

Chapter 5

It is so true that sometimes one has to make a sacrifice for the greater good.

I have slept for the past week with the cream shawl on my bed. I didn't have it lying beside my head on the same pillow, that would have creased and disturbed it and made it smell of me. No, I smoothed it over the spare pillow beside me. At night as I have drifted off to sleep, I have been able to stroke and caress the soft fine fabric and the smooth fringes. During the day I kept it safely folded in a vacuum sealed bag to preserve the faint perfume clinging to its folds. Oh, what a treasure it has been. After a week, though, the perfume is all but dissipated and although still serving as a memento, it is of less value to me and I've decided that it could be put to better use.

I did some small investigation on the net in a calmer frame of mind than the first day that I saw her. With a more logical approach it took less than ten minutes to find the web site. At my fingertips I had the telephone number and details of Hummingbird, Interior Design and the name and details of the director. This was my way in. Returning the shawl would deprive myself of that small pleasure in the night but it could take me into the very presence of my heart's desire.

I took it with me, carefully protected in a linen pillowcase, and walked down to the old Victorian building. My heart pounded with a passion hard to describe. I was about to meet and speak to my angel.

After ringing the bell, a faint scratchy voice answered. I announced quite simply "I have your shawl." I realised afterwards that it may not have been my dear Hummingbird and all could have gone wrong but luck was with me.

"Oh, how wonderful. Come on up." She didn't know how those few words made my heart sing. The door clicked, allowing entrance to her sphere.

The Hummingbird office is on the third floor. The building is well maintained and smart. The clouded glass window carries the legend, Hummingbird Interior Design and underneath Hannah Bird - Director.

I pushed open the heavy wooden door and walked into a small reception area. As the door closed behind me, she came from her office. Smiling and holding out her hand she could not possibly know how she was affecting me. My heart pounded and my head swam. I took her hand, the skin was soft and smooth,

I felt the tiny bones that I had watched so often flicking at the cigarettes and lifting the coffee cups to her lips. It was surreal to be so close, to be touching her.

I held out the little parcel, "I found this on the street, just by the corner. When I enquired at Costa, they said that they thought it was yours. I haven't had the chance to come this way until now."

"That is so very kind of you to bother." Her voice was soft and mellow, she spoke calmly and all about her was perfect as I always knew it would be. She drew the shawl from its bag and threw it around her shoulders.

"I am so pleased to have this back. It was a gift from a very dear friend. I stupidly left it on the back of a chair outside the coffee shop and it must have blown off and down the street. Thank you so very much Miss or is it Mrs… erm?"

"Jobson, Amy Jobson, and you are very welcome, it was no trouble at all. I am happy that you have it back."

"Will you let me take you for a cup of coffee as a thank you? Or lunch – how about that? It is just about time for me to break for an hour. Would you let me treat you to lunch in the bistro on the corner?"

All my dreams have come true. We have met and now we are to have our first meal together. My cup really does run over with happiness.

Chapter 6

She sits opposite to me, the sunlight shining on the highlights in her hair. The spun golden strands dance at the sides of her head. Her eyes, an unusual grey and blue mix, are large and clear. The skin at the corners crinkles slightly, she smiles often and the smile lights her eyes and imprints the skin of her face. I adore that about her, that she carries the proof of her good nature for the world to witness. Her lips are full and curve upwards slightly at the corners as she talks to me of incidentals. There are two quite large dark freckles just to the side of her nose and one more on the side of her chin. Her skin is smooth and fine. She is a living masterpiece.

As we wait for our meal my glance is drawn to her fascinating hands. They are long and slender and the skin stretches tautly over those impossibly fragile bones. Her nails are short but not as neat as one would have expected, there is evidence that she chews them occasionally – so the elegance of the first day was false. I find this tiny fault endearing, a sign of deep emotions; worries maybe. If she would only let me, I would take care of all her worries, calm all her fears. My own little Hummingbird. If only she knew how she affected me now in this ordinary, rather boring place. If she could only discern how my heart pounds and flutters and my hands are damp with the excitement of being so close. At this thought I glance at my own hands, lying as hers are atop the wooden table. My nails are manicured and neat but ah how dark, how rough my skin when compared to hers, how plain and ordinary they look. I am ashamed of their ordinariness and fold them on my lap out of sight where they belong.

I am so overcome with the moment that I have let her do all the talking. Now I think she is wondering about me and my silence. I drag my thoughts back. What was she saying just now, before my mind wandered to the perfection of her hands? Ah yes, the workaday world, how incongruous to talk of such stuff with her but I must.

"My work, oh, rather boring, I'm afraid. Computer stuff, web design and such like. Not as glamorous as interior design must be."

"Oh, I should think that it is very interesting, all jobs have their boring side, of course, and I have to say that parts of mine are very humdrum and dull."

"Is it your own business?"

That was it, those few words were the end of joy.

"No, not really, I am in partnership with my husband." The world spun, the day was dulled and for one moment my mind was an empty void. I had never for one moment even considered that she may have a husband. I realise now it was stupid of me but such was my belief in the rightness of our future together that I could imagine no other person would have claim to her.

Chapter 7

The beauty is gone from the day. The warmth of the sun through the window is chilled and the aroma of food cooking, which only moments ago caused me to salivate, now causes mild nausea and disgust. I want to leave. It is a struggle for me to sit on this hard, wooden chair. I notice for the first time that there is a greasy spot on the wooden arm and salt has been spilled, which no-one has cleaned from the tabletop.

She is chatting still, now I see that her arms wave and gesticulate unnecessarily to accompany her dialogue. I can form no rational thoughts. My mind is full of this new and devastating knowledge. She has a husband; she is a wife. Another person has shared and will share her most private moments. He has held her body and caressed it, kissed those lips which only moments before I had admired. I can't let my mind walk that pathway; it will drive me to distraction. I nod and smile and try to cover my confusion but after a little while she pauses in her chatter.

"My dear, are you quite well? You have suddenly gone terribly pale. Can I have them fetch you a drink of water. Do you need some air?"

I shake my head and raise my hand to fend off the kind gesture which, if allowed, will call forth tears I know it.

"I'm fine, really, a momentary dizziness, it's nothing. I am probably hungry. I wonder how long the food will be."

I am rescued by the waitress delivering a plate of sawdust for me to struggle through. It is supposed to be a chicken and pasta dish. The chicken is dry and overcooked and the pasta is badly prepared but I force it into my mouth and swallow it hardly chewed. I drink my wine; I don't normally drink alcohol at lunchtime but this was my celebration and it deserved the sparkling recognition we were to give it. My head is floating unattached above my shoulders and my arms and legs are made of rubber.

What the hell, I give way to the sensations and allow myself to watch from afar as she twirls pasta and breaks bread to dip into the bloody sauce. She has broken my soul and made worthless my life. She has no idea and talks on, enjoying this small deviation from her normal day. A couple of times she looks concerned and flashes a questioning glance. I force myself to react with a smile and a raised glass, and the occasion passes. I am in a torturous hell where my heart screams and cracks unseen and unremarked upon by my assassin.

Despite my efforts she realises that all is not well with me. She reaches across the table and lays a gentle hand over mine. What is left of my heart fractures into a thousand pieces.

"Are you alright? What's wrong? Please let's just leave, you are dreadfully pale. Let me take you home."

I nod and allow her to pay the bill with only the smallest of dispute for appearances sake and we leave. As we reach the step, she takes my arm and steadies me. This touch should fill me with ecstasy but it scorches my skin. This hand holds his, this hand caresses his body and look now, this hand does not wear his ring, though surely it should!

Chapter 8

Her kindness is limitless. She closes her office, drives me home and supports me with a steadying arm as we walk up my narrow path. I fumble with the rock hiding the key and she takes it from me to unlock the door.

It is cool and welcoming in my home and now she is here. Her perfume is in the air of these rooms. Slipping off her shoes at the door she patters to the kitchen, bare skin slapping on ceramic. The rattle of the water into the kettle intrudes as I sit at the table stunned by her being here. The small slam of my cupboard doors, chinking and ringing of crockery, the shush of the fridge and then the aroma of brewing coffee. Her presence here in my space heightens every sense. The smell of the brew is overwhelming as the coffee steams in the small cup she places before me. There is a biscuit from the tin placed on the saucer.

"Here. Some sugar, caffeine. This will help, you should eat. Drink the coffee."

It scalds my tongue and throat, I gasp.

"Oh God, sorry I should have put some cold in. Are you alright?"

"Yes, yes, don't worry. Please don't worry. You are being so kind, there really is no need. I am not ill, truly I am not ill."

"But you went so pale, I thought for a moment you were going to faint. Do you have diabetes maybe, something like that? You should check, you know, see the doctor. It's best to find out. Just in case you know."

"Truly, my dear, I am really fine. To be perfectly honest I had some bad news and I think that it simply hit me harder than is reasonable."

"Oh, you poor thing. Nothing too horrible, was it? I am sorry, and you being so kind, bringing back my shawl. You could have sent it you know. I really do appreciate what you did."

"No, truly I am fine. I am simply being rather silly and dramatic for no reason. Thank you for bringing me home and making the drink and really just for being so patient."

Her eyes light in a smile and she bends to wrap her arms around me in a tender hug. "You know, I really like you. I think that we could be friends." The blush creeps into her cheeks, wiping years from her face, and she grins. "Oh, would you listen to me, I sound like a kid. It's just that you are so friendly and I feel so very comfortable with you. It seems as though we have known each other for years. I can't believe that we've only just met."

"Well, I have to say that pleases me and I know just what you mean. I would really consider it a privilege if you would let me return the favour. Well actually if you would let me make amends for today's rather spoiled lunch. Do you think it would be alright for us to have dinner sometime, perhaps? Will that cause any sort of problem for you at home?"

"Home?"

"Yes, you know with your husband. Or maybe there are children, babysitters to arrange."

"Oh no, sorry, I didn't mean to give the impression… well, the thing is we aren't together anymore. Divorced. But the business, well that was easier to just leave things like that. We are friends, well sort of and no there are no children. I would love to have dinner with you, Amy, I really would."

My world glows with rainbows as it begins to spin again. She smiles at me and sips the cooling coffee.

Chapter 9

She is gone and my rooms have become voids. The silence resounds and I feel that I will be lost in the empty spaces. When departing, on the drive she paused and turned and blew a kiss – an old-fashioned and charming gesture that took my breath, leaving me gasping from emptied lungs. The great car, a leviathan in black with glittering chrome and darkened windows, a monster of a thing was made wonderful by her hands at the wheel and her slender feet against the pedals. It drew away from the kerb and I watched until it turned at the corner and became a memory.

The door slammed into the silence and I leaned my back to the wood and slid, slowly and ungraciously to the floor. Hugging myself in delight and disbelief I replayed every moment of this chaotic, desperate, storm laden day. From the ghastly discovery of a husband and the dreadful bistro meal to the wondrous parade of events that brought her here to my home, my kitchen, sitting at my table.

As I loll against the wood, surrounded by the ticking of my great clock and the creaking of central heating, the day gives way to evening. The shadows grow and the familiar noises of returning commuters drag me back to reality and to the need to move lest the numbness in my legs renders me lame. I don't want to limp; I don't want to feel my age. She is young, so very much younger than I am, with a lithe and supple body and shining hair. Passing the hall stand I avert my eyes from the mirror. Wrinkles, sagging skin and dulled eyes have never bothered me until I start to imagine how she sees me. As her mother, her grandmother surely not, but then again, just what is the age difference? Turning back, I approach the glass that gleams in the fading daylight. There it is, my old face, the creases and wrinkles undeniable. My hair styled for practicality rather than glamour and my eyes, are they rheumy behind my sensible spectacles?

The sobbing starts before I even acknowledge the sadness, and useless tears cascade across my flabby cheeks. I rub at the moisture and try to control the outburst. Where has this come from, could I really be ill? No, of course not. I am overwrought by the events of the last few hours and more, so much more than that I am reduced by the knowledge that my dear Hummingbird is most probably beyond my grasp. Cruel. Cruel that I should meet her now in the gloaming of my days. I know that she is so much more than I could have ever hoped but at the same moment I acknowledge that she is, for me, so very, very far out of reach.

I banister drag myself up the stairs and throw myself across the duvet and give way to a torrent of self-pity and hopelessness. For the first time in my life I feel the years crushing me and I wail for the past and for the loss and for the pain of it all.

Chapter 10

Tonight, we will meet again for dinner. This is the third date and I am dressing with care. I apply cosmetics, something that I thought I had forsaken for good some years ago but Hannah insists that I should "Keep up my standards." Not give up on the feminine side of things. I call her Hannah; I have let go the pretension of Hummingbird. She is so much more real now and is deserving of her correct title. She is Hannah and in the secret corners of my mind I admit that she is "My Hannah".

We are going to an Italian restaurant and then to a play reading. Friends from when I taught at the college part-time have invited us. More properly they invited me and a friend, and what other friend would I take? She is endearingly excited about the play reading; it is her first experience of such and I pray that she won't be disappointed. I am so very surprised at her naivety. For such an accomplished businesswoman and talented artist, she is surprisingly inexperienced in many things that I have taken for granted. She has travelled a little and is "cultured" in the usual sort of way, some Shakespeare, opera even -- Glyndebourne with her ex-husband – but there are still many, many things for me to show her, and indeed she teaches me something new every time we meet.

We are comfortable together now; her sense of humour is perforce younger than mine but it is enchanting to me. I have yet to broach the subject of the difference in our ages, I don't dare mention it. I have chosen to ignore it. It is a pretence and I know it will come back to haunt me and I continually shore up the wall that threatens to crumble each time I acknowledge the issue. I am afraid all the time, I fear that she will tire of me, that she will realise that there are too many differences, that the generational discrepancy will prove too much. So many things that keep me tossing and turning in the night, and in an agony of worry in the day when my mind insists that I think about it. So many things that could force my hand and cause me to act while I am still unprepared.

For tonight I will live again in the moment, I will enjoy the sight of her, the feel of her skin as she wraps her arms around me. I will devour the wondrous feel of her lips on my cheek and the brush of air as she kisses me. I will enjoy the tinkle of her voice, the chime of her laughter and the warmth of her in my space. I will bathe in the glory of her nearness. Then later when I am alone again I will, I know, feel the track of saltwater across my cheeks and under my ears as I lie in my solitary bed and crave her presence.

It can't go on, I know that the time is coming when I will have to decide how to progress, what direction this relationship will take. Will she come willingly, become my happy helpmate and my loving companion or will it be like the last time, the time with Marie. I pray there will be no need for any of that and as my thoughts stray down that painful alleyway, I fiddle with the charm on my neck chain. It is the only thing that there is left of her – my silly, silly girl. How sad that was.

Chapter 11

The days move on and with them joy grows ever stronger. I have invited Hannah for dinner. I am in a dither; my hands shake as I trim beans and skin the salmon. The wine is chilled and there are small dishes of nuts and dips with carrot sticks. Flowers cascade in colourful abandon from vases on the side tables and my room is shadowed and charming with the small lights turned on and the curtains closed. I love my home and have spent many hours and much money on the gathering of things and the decoration. Normally it is a source of great pride but tonight I see only the faults. There are stains on the wall near the door, the result of damp umbrellas leaning there. There is a crack on one of the kitchen tiles, which I have never been able to have repaired. These small things bother me occasionally but tonight they have assumed huge importance. Her life is, after all, made up of decoration and beautification.

The times that she has visited, since the first time when she made coffee, she has merely rung the bell and I have been ready, waiting for her in a fever of anticipation, so we have left with only a momentary greeting. There is sound reason for this. I don't think I can trust myself alone in my home with her. I have no confidence in my ability to hold my tongue and not blurt out my feelings and my desires. It has been too soon, I know, so I have avoided a situation that would lead me astray and cause untimely action.

Now I am ready, the time has come. I can wait no longer. I have no way to gauge what her reactions and indeed her actions will be. I know that she was married but she has shown great affection for me and often hugs and kisses me. She is naturally a very tactile person, to my continuous delight I admit. Anyway, I have made the decision, tonight I will lay my cards on the table. I will admit my total devotion to her and if I judge that it is time to progress my case, I will suggest that we take our relationship to another level. It is dangerous, it is nerve-wracking; it is an end game for I will have her, and tonight will decide how and when that will happen.

The time approaches, the clock chimes six and I hear her great car pull in to the kerb. I hear the click clack of her heels on my path. There it is, the chime of the doorbell. I throw my apron onto the worktop. I check my appearance in the hall mirror.

"Welcome, my dear, welcome." A short peck on the cheek.

"Some wine, I hope it will suit what we are eating."

"Perfect, quite perfect. Come in, here let me take your coat."

I lock the door and take the key and slip it into the little wooden drawer, she doesn't see. She walks before me down the dimly lit hall.

Chapter 12

Well, I don't know, I just don't know. I had thought deeply about how the evening might progress. It is my own fault, I know, but how was I to help it? Such hopes had bloomed as I planned and prepared. It is too soon, I see that now, but how deep is this disappointment?

In my mind I had foreseen a pleasant evening leading to my declaration and her happy, happy acceptance. Perhaps talk of the future, at the least a deepening of our connection.

It began well, the food was… adequate, the atmosphere convivial and intimate. Music filled the quiet moments. Hannah truly did seem to enjoy what she ate and she is a delightful table companion. My standards are high, there is a correct way to behave at table and although there are a few rough edges there she performed well. I can polish and hone her until our future meals together will be the delight I have missed for so long.

Perhaps it has been too long, perhaps my voluntary solitude has made me too friable, too intense. I never expected that she would stay the night, of course not. Indeed it would have been in some way a disappointment, an indication of looser morals than I would hope for.

The last years have been difficult, I have needed to work so very hard. Maria, how you still hurt me. True, it hasn't always been so very near to the forefront of my mind but it is there, like a miasma hidden in the more solid everyday. I try to hold it back, I keep busy, physical activity is often the answer.

I take other precautions as well. Sensible adult actions. I never go to the woods at the top of the Heath. I know that should I go there; my feet would be drawn inexorably to that spot where the earth is soft and the moss smells of damp and rot. That way lies disaster. I never see any of our old acquaintances. This is easy as I moved away from our old flat after the event. I don't play the music that she liked, I have discarded many discs and films that we listened to and watched together. Yes, I decided very quickly that the best way to insulate myself was to try to behave as if the whole sad, sad affair had never happened. But it did, didn't it? So now and again when my guard is down, she intrudes. It has made me afraid, afraid to hope and to trust, I couldn't bear it should I find myself in that place again.

No, no I don't need to go down that road. I had dreaded that something of that nature would happen but, in the event, we spent a wonderful evening of friendship and laughter and before I could take things any further it was time for her to go. As we stood in the hall waiting for the taxi, I took her hand ready to declare myself and she simply smiled and leaned to me and kissed me lightly on the cheek.

"What a lovely evening we have had. You must come to me next time and we must make it soon." And at that the taxi blew its horn and she was gone. I felt bereft and stupid to be frank and even now can't explain how I let things get so much away from me.

Now I am sitting here unwilling to go upstairs, I know that tonight Maria will be with me. I have a feeling of dread and a solid lump of disquiet in my stomach. I will need to remain sleepless, on guard. I will do some work and then, if that doesn't help, there is no other option but to go and run in the dark streets with the rain glistening on the cobbles and the silence of the night to wrap up my thoughts and deaden the memory.

Chapter 13

I have tried to work but the wine will have its way and no meaningful progress will be made tonight.

It feels strange to be donning running gear with the streetlamps peering through the gaps in the curtains and the house creaking in the way that houses only do in the darkest hours. I feel a thrill, I am not afraid, I will take a whistle with me and my confidence and all will be well.

As I pull the door closed quietly behind me, the damp air kisses my cheek and moisture very quickly coats the skin of my face. There is the feel of rain in the air and the trees drip quietly into the silence.

Down the path and turn, to the left. No, tonight I will take the other route. The wine fizzes in my blood and my nerves tingle as I head for the Heath. I shouldn't do this, I know, but there is madness in me now. Where did it come from? I don't know, but it enthrals me and the decision is made to let it draw me onwards down roads that I have avoided for some two years. Up the once familiar slope to the top of the Heath and then across the gravel and there it is before me now – the wood.

Shivers trickle up and down my spine as my pulse quickens more from the strange excitement than from the jogging. Oh, I know I am no longer young but I have stayed fit, partly because of good genes and partly because of effort. The exercise has taken very little toll on my breathing but this thing that I am about to do causes my lungs to feel deprived and my heart to thud in a way that is part discomfort, part thrill. My knees shake, and my hands tremble.

The branches are lowered with the weight of the rain on the leaves and they grab and reach at me as I enter the darkness. There is no need for a torch. The moonlight and the small glow from the streetlamps are enough. Although I haven't been this way for many months, I know the pathway as if I trod it only yesterday. I have imagined this journey over and over. The weight of the body, the stickiness of the drying blood and yes, I admit it, the horror of what I had done. It has become now like a dream or a film seen many years ago but as I tread deeper along the spongy path the night transforms and I am transported in time. I can almost see it from this two-year distance, her head lolls against my shoulder, her body, wrapped in a sheet is surprisingly heavy and I stop several times to rest. The fear comes back, much diminished but still it clenches at my gut and causes me to gasp. I hadn't forgotten but I now remember vividly and it is more awful than I had thought.

It is deeply dark now and I need to hold my hand in front of me to avoid colliding with the trunks and take care that I don't trip on partly buried roots. That night I had brought a torch because I had gone back and forth, once with the bundle in the sheet and then back for the spade from the boot of the car, and then lastly for the small bag of belongings that I needed to dispose of.

It is there now before me, the clearing. How peaceful it seems. Quiet in the gloom – just shadow and yet deeper shadow; with here and there the glow of a white rock or a piece of litter. I think I remember the very tree and slowly I approach. Yes, yes this is the one. It is a huge willow and at the base I know that the rich soil and green moss are imbued with decay.

My knees have at last let me go and I flop to the earth, I am overwhelmed with feelings I don't understand. It is a strange passion, recognition of the magnitude of the deed and then atop that relief that all is as it was – there is no sign of disturbance and I realise that this has been cathartic for me. It has actually been beneficial to come here and be where she is.

"Maria, how different it could all have been."

Chapter 14

I sat for quite some time beside the great tree. The rain stopped and although the trees dripped and the grass dampened my jogging pants, it was peaceful. For the first time in two years I allowed the horror of that dreadful night to invade my thoughts.

Ah, Maria. I had believed that she was the answer to my loneliness, she was young, yes, and so she was fresh and new. She was charming and a little flighty. Her blonde beauty took my breath whenever I watched her moving and laughing and living.

I remembered how the connection between us had grown from the time when we met in the queue in the supermarket. She had never known how I had watched her, worshipping her from a distance for weeks. How I had waited outside the hospital until she came off duty and how I had paced back and forth along the road where her little flat was, just for a momentary glimpse as she walked to her car.

As the relationship grew, we had taken meals together in the little cafés near her home. We had visited bars near to the hospital and all the time I had nursed the idea that we would make a life together. She moved in with me as a lodger and then after a week of bliss I judged the time ready for my declaration.

That dreadful night. The nightmare of it all came back and as I sat on the damp grass, I heard her laughter again and the mocking words with which she cruelly rejected my advances. I heard again the crack as the heavy lamp connected with the bones of her skull and the soft shushing as her limp body crumpled to the floor.

Oh my God, I cried for the horror of it all there in the dripping woodland. I cried for the fear, the panic and the grief. I shook like the quivering leaves above me as I re-lived the desperation and the enormity of my actions. I sobbed as I remembered what I had done to preserve my existence. I had wrapped the still-warm body. Collecting the few belongings that she had moved into the little bedroom I left my house with her for the nightmare drive to the Heath. I dug in the dark woods. Now I imagined I could hear again the heavy thud her body made as it rolled over the heap of earth I had piled beside the shallow hole.

I stopped my mad mind race. I drew a deep breath and I stood. For a moment I bowed my head in sorrow. There was no use for this so I straightened my shoulders, stiffened my spine and turned away.

Oh yes, I feel so very much better, so I jog back towards my home. Through the wood and the Heath and down the shimmering streets. As my feet pound the damp flagstones, I feel a new resolve growing. I will handle things differently this time. My dearest Hannah, with you I will be sure to judge my time better. I am glad now that I haven't spoken yet. Providence was with me last night, oh yes. All is well and my heart is light as I approach my road.

I see that the massive car is still in my drive and as I draw nearer, I see that Hannah has come to collect it. She is climbing into the driving seat and I raise a hand to wave, to catch her eye. That is when I notice that there is another figure in the car, a passenger in the other seat. Another woman, I think. At this time in the morning who is this with her in the predawn light? Here she is collecting her car like a thief in the night and with a collaborator.

Chapter 15

I am puzzled and uneasy. Was she trying to avoid meeting me? Surely not after the wonderful evening we spent. More importantly, though, who was the passenger in the other seat?

As I take my shower, I mull those moments and what I had seen over and over until I doubt the evidence of my own eyes. I know that the car has gone so there is solid proof that I did indeed see Hannah but was it a trick of the dull light and shadow that made it appear that there was another figure inside? My mind whirls and my nerves jangle with perturbation. I must take control. Stepping out of the needling water I use a harsh towel to rub my body until it is pink and humming. Downstairs the watery light through my kitchen window shines on my scalding cup of coffee as I sit at the table trying to concentrate.

I have spent a very emotional and highly charged night. No sleep, rather an excess of alcohol and the turmoil in my soul caused by the visit to the wood.

In truth I know so very little about her life. I had taken it as read that Hannah lives alone. She tells me that she is divorced but continues to run the interior design business with her ex-husband. I assumed that she occupies the flat that she has, off the London Road by the hospital, alone.

To date I have not declared my interest. The times that we have spent together have been as loving friends. She knows nothing of when I possessed her shawl, those wonderful nights when it lay across the pillow on my bed and I caressed it and smoothed it as I drifted into sleep. Tears start to my eyes at the thought that there is someone else who shares her life.

I think that the shape in the car was female. Oh, how cruel that would be for me to find that there is another love interest and that it should be someone like myself who appreciates Hannah's beauty and femininity. Someone who treats her with gentle care as I would if only I were to be given the opportunity.

I am bereft and my mind races this way and that; I am unable to catch a thought and pin it down. My hands shake and the coffee splashes onto the tabletop. Roughly I push back the chair and it tumbles to the floor scratching the front of the cupboard. I pace back and forth across the tiles; my hands wring and tears escape to trace lines across my cheeks.

I take a deep breath. I declare aloud, "Stop now, stop it." I stand before the window and allow my brain to settle, my thoughts to calm. I will go now, today. I will find the flat in the street off London Road and I will watch. It is something I do well. I will find a place from where to keep vigil, a place where I am invisible and I will watch and when I see the truth then I will make my plan.

I leave the house and take my bicycle and ride through the quiet roads, round by the park and then down to the London Road. I have her address on a piece of paper. It is so easy now to find addresses on the internet. Just a couple of minutes is all it took me. I can see it opposite to me, the converted Victorian mansion and in the front parking area the great black car. Now, my love, now I will watch you like a guardian angel.

Chapter 16

Five days have passed since the night that I spent in the woods with my memories and Maria. I have watched for most of that time hidden in a dark corner near to the house where Hannah has her flat. There is a church almost opposite with an imposing gateway. The stone pillars are tall and wide and the pathway overhung with a dark growth of trees and shrubs. It is perfect for me.

I suppose that in years gone by I could not have used that place, churches were visited daily and I would be continually in danger of being seen. Now, though, apart from scavenging dogs and one or two old ladies with sad little bunches of flowers there is no passing traffic. The old ladies barely glanced at me, there is a war memorial just beside the pathway and I made a great pretence of reading the names inscribed in the stone.

From my secret place I was able to see Hannah's flat very clearly. I was there in the morning before she woke. She rises at around seven. The first day I was there from four because I didn't know her routine but after that I was able to arrive between six and seven.

The light in what I have discovered must be her bedroom flashes on behind the flimsy cream curtains. It is a small light and I imagine it to be some sort of alarm clock, probably one of those which turn on the radio. Does she listen to music as she wakes or is it the news that starts her day? So much for me to discover about her. There is a small window beside the bedroom. The glass is frosted so it must be the bathroom. The first morning I was overwhelmed by what I saw. The flat is on the second floor and so it must feel very private – my beautiful girl comes to the kitchen window in the early morning light. Her hair is dishevelled from tossing in her sleep. The light is behind her and her head is alight with the golden strands of unkempt hair. Quite, quite beautiful. Each day she has worn a gown with thin straps and as my eye lights on her almost bare shoulders I imagine the feel of that skin; I anticipate when I am able to caress it and enfold her in my arms.

For three of the days she left quite early and climbed into her car to head into town. I pedalled quickly through the back streets and was able to arrive very shortly after she did at her little office in the old building near to Costa. I stayed in town all day watching in case she went out or met anyone and then repeated the trip in reverse to see her turning on her lights as she arrived back at her home.

I am far, far behind in my work. Two deadlines have passed unfilled and I have many calls needing to be returned, but for now it must all wait. My house has grown dusty and there is no fresh food left in the fridge. I can't spare the time to shop. Should I turn my back for a moment, I could miss her meeting with someone or leaving her work for a lunch time dalliance. I can't risk any time away from where she is.

The other days were a worry to me, she rose at the usual time and then stayed in the flat for longer. Eventually driving away, she headed in the other direction and off towards the motorway. Of course it was impossible for me to follow then and I spent the days in agony wondering where she was and what she was doing.

However, one thing is now clear to me, and I can hardly contain my delight – she does indeed live alone.

I have watched her walk from room to room, stand by the window and pull the heavy curtains at night and always it is she and she alone who I have seen. One day another person arrived just after she had gone into the flat. It was a woman who rang the bell. Hannah came to the door and invited her inside. It didn't cause me any discomfort because it was clear that although they did seem to know each other, there was no real affection evident in the greetings and the visitor stayed about an hour before leaving on foot.

My worries were for nothing. She is alone in her life so when I make my move there will be nothing and no-one for her to worry and wonder about. The relief I feel is overwhelming.

I have called her today; I have invited her to a play and for dinner tomorrow evening and she has told me that she will let me know by this afternoon. I don't know why she couldn't agree immediately, there can be no reason for her not to come. I have seen her life; it is quiet and really I think rather empty. Well not for much longer, my dear Hannah. I intend to fill every moment of your future with my love.

She can give up the flat, I imagine that it is rented and there is no need for her to keep it on. She will come here, of course. I did consider preparing the smaller bedroom but held off for now. She might well want to bring some of her own things and then together we will set up our home. I am so happy for her, she is as yet unaware of my plans for us, but how can she fail to be anything but delighted when I set it all before her?

I have bought a nightdress like the one that she wears. It is wrapped in tissue in one of the empty drawers just waiting. I have been rather silly and bought some of the perfume that she uses, this is in the drawer also. I have been able to find a shawl just like hers and I use it now when I sit and read in bed. It makes me feel close to her and I have sprayed it with the perfume. I can almost believe that she is here with me already.

Chapter 17

The strains of Beethoven ring out from my mobile. I am always shocked when it sounds, in fact I am going to change it to a more ordinary ringtone. I had thought it was quirky and modern of me to have it sound music but now I have to confess that it doesn't suit me. Pressing the tiny button my heart jumps as I see the message on the screen, Hannah calling.

"Hannah, my dear. How are you?"

"Fine, yes just fine, Amy. I am calling about the play, about tonight."

"Ah, you are coming, aren't you?"

"Yes, yes that's it. I am really looking forward to it. Shall we eat before or after, it may be quite late?"

"I did wonder, my dear. How about we eat afterwards and then maybe you could come back here with me and spend the night. I could make up the spare room and you would be very welcome."

"Well, your place is about the same distance from town as mine. I don't see that it would save any time."

I must think quickly, she must come, she must.

"Oh, I thought that we could eat at the new French place that has opened and it is nearer to me. If you don't want to, that's okay, I'll cancel the booking."

"Oh, gosh no, no I didn't realize you had gone to such trouble. No, no that's fine."

"I thought that we could eat and then come back here for a nightcap and you won't have to worry about driving or anything."

"Well, it seems a bit, erm…"

"Look, don't let me force you. I realize that you have a very busy life and that it may be a bit of a bother for you." I play on her sympathy; I try to pull at her gentle nature.

"Amy please don't be upset."

Is it working, my ploy?

"Of course I will come and stay, it will be lovely. I'll come to you about seven in the car and then we can take a taxi to the theatre and be relaxed about it all. I hope I haven't offended you."

"No, I'm not offended my dear. I don't want to be a bother to you."

"Oh, Amy you could never be a bother. I'm looking forward to tonight. It will make a lovely change and then in the morning I'll treat you to breakfast in town."

She is coming. She will be here with me in my space for a whole glorious night. We will wake together in the morning. I don't want to go out to breakfast but judged that I had argued against her enough. There will be the opportunity to change that plan in due course.

I am in a state of absolute bliss. The room is polished and shining, there are fresh flowers in a bowl on the dresser. I have made up the bed with soft cotton bedding and sprayed her perfume lightly on the pillow. The new gown is spread across the bed. She will be so surprised when she finds the preparations I have made for her. Champagne is in the fridge. I can't settle, can't sit still.

Tonight can't come fast enough. The clock ticks slowly counting the endless hours until we meet. I toss clothes across my room trying to decide what to wear. I have a wonderful sense of anticipation; my life will be changed after tonight. I shall have a companion, a house mate and a loving friend. Oh, I know that it may take a little while to persuade her that I am right but once she is here and sees how well I can care for her, how simple I can make her life then all will be well.

The biggest surprise, though, will be the room at the top of the house. I have converted it into the most wonderful office and studio for her. I have installed all the things that she needs. I have studied her web site in great depth and the pictures of her office. I have copied them, blown them up and researched all that I saw. I have reproduced it entirely, she will be so thrilled. She will never have to go to town, she can stay here with me. I will work in my office and there she will be just above my head working in hers.

Chapter 18

"Come in, come in. Let me take your coat. Please go through to the sitting room. Make yourself comfortable, Hannah, my home is your home as the Spanish say."

"Thank you, Amy. It is always so lovely and cosy in here, and look at all these beautiful flowers."

"Let me just fetch our drinks. You would like some Champagne surely, wouldn't you?"

"Wonderful, it feels like a celebration."

"Yes, well I feel that it is in a way. Let me bring it through and then we can be cosy and talk."

I am in the kitchen and she calls through to me.

"What did you think of the play, Amy? I thought it was a little slow to start but it picked up."

I have to raise my voice to answer. I really don't like to have conversations in this fashion. I must be sure to let her know that. It is best, I think, to start as we mean to go on so there are no misunderstandings.

"Oh Moet, how lovely and what pretty glasses! I always feel that you live much more graciously than I do, Amy, it's really very special to be here."

"I am so glad you feel that way. I really was hoping that we could have quite a serious chat actually."

"Oh, my goodness you do look solemn, Amy. There's nothing wrong is there?"

"No, no. Here we are. Cheers my dear, here's to friendship and love."

"Oh, erm… well, yes, of course."

I move to sit beside her on the sofa, she shifts away and leans against the arm. I can sense a tension in her demeanour. I must relax the atmosphere. Music! Yes, of course. I turn on the sound system and the room is flooded with the sounds of Mozart. I retake my seat and sip at the cool, sparkling wine. I am in heaven.

"Hannah. You do know, don't you, how much I value your friendship?"

She shuffles a little beside me. She is tense, her back is a ramrod and her fingers twiddle and play with the stem of the champagne glass. I must get on with this and not allow the mood to sour.

"I have never known anyone quite like you, my dear. I find you fascinating."

She laughs a little, a small sound that is in some strange way dismissive. "Amy, I'm sorry, you are making me uncomfortable." She places her glass on the table, the condensation runs and pools on the polish. She really will need to take care of the furnishings.

Now I have to fetch a napkin from the kitchen and take a coaster from the little basket.

I take my seat again. "Where was I? Ah yes. I really feel that there is something special between us, Hannah. You must feel that also; you do, don't you?"

"I like you very much, Amy, of course. I really enjoyed this evening, I did, but to be honest I am wondering if I ought to go home. It's not as late as I thought it would be and really it would be more convenient. Why don't I just finish this drink and then I will see you tomorrow? We could have lunch?"

"No, no don't be silly. Lunch. I don't want to have lunch. You must stay, you said you would." I grasp her hand and pull her to her feet. "Come and see, come and see what I have done, the effort I have gone to. Lunch. How could you even suggest going back to your flat?"

"Amy, let go of me. Let go of my arm. What on earth do you think you're doing?"

"Come with me, come upstairs. It's all prepared."

She snatches her arm away and bends to retrieve her evening bag from the side stand. "I think I should just go home. It seems that maybe there has been some sort of misunderstanding here, Amy. I only agreed to stay because you seemed to want it so much. Amy, please understand, I like you as a friend but if I have given you any sort of idea that there was anything more than that. My God, how could you think that? I don't know how this has happened but I must be clear I am not interested in anything more than friendship. I am not like that, Amy, not– well, not that way at all. I had no idea that you were, well, that you..."

"That I what, what is it that you are saying? You must have felt the chemistry between us."

"No. For heaven's sake. No."

She stands and turns to me, her face flushed. She clutches the little bag before her as if it were a shield. Tears have come unbidden to my eyes and through the mist I see the look on her face. She is horrified. I have seen that look before. No, this must not happen again.

She turns to leave with just a glance backwards. I must act now; I know that if she were to leave now, I will never see her again. I can't bear it; the thought is a knife in my guts. Through the lump of pain in my throat I manage to speak.

"Wait, wait please, Hannah." She turns. "Wait, I'm sorry, please, I have made a mistake. I really do apologise but please don't go, sit down now have another drink. Please let us just talk. I understand, truly I do, and your friendship is so valuable to me please let's just talk."

She looks into my face and as her expression softens, she raises her hand slightly towards me and a small smile touches the corners of her beautiful lips.

"Oh Amy, how sad this is. You are so sweet and I have really enjoyed spending time with you. Here sit down, sit back down, here's your drink. Don't be upset now. I am sure we can sort this out. I didn't realize what was happening but I am sure we can still be friends."

Relief floods my system; I am weakened by it. "Oh Hannah. You really are wonderful."

"Sit down, come on let's talk. I am sorry; I didn't know you were hoping for more than for us to be friends. Is there no-one for you? Have you never had a, well, a partner?"

Should I tell her? The champagne is tickling at my brain. I feel unresolved. Should I tell her some of it? It would be wonderful to share.

"Well, yes there was someone once. I had a friend. She was younger than I. Her name was Maria."

"Oh, what happened, why are you not together now?"

I take a breath. "She died, Hannah, she is gone."

A hand flies to her mouth as she gasps. "How awful. Amy I am so very sorry I really am. When was this, when did she die? Was she ill, an accident? Oh, my goodness. Maybe you don't want to talk about it."

"Yes, an accident. That's it, there was a terrible accident."

Chapter 19

She is here, she is in my home. We talked long into the night and climbed the stairs together. I was circumspect at the bedroom door. I simply touched her arm and wished her pleasant dreams. I know, yes, I know that just now she is a little unnerved and unsure but the first part of the plan has been accomplished.

In the night, when the moon sailed amongst the clouds and my world was quiet and still, I went to her room. I trod along the landing with great care. The glassware lining the windowsills glowed with the silver moonlight and the dark shadows of great trees painted mobiles on the walls.

There are no locks on my internal doors. I have never felt the need for them. I gently turned the knob and stepped over the threshold into paradise. She lay quite still; the bedding was barely disturbed. Her hair tumbled in a gleaming wave across the pillow and her skin was kissed and burnished by the gentle glow through the voile curtains. Black lashes lay against the smooth alabaster of her cheeks and her hand curled like a seashell beside her head. I listened to her breathing, the waves of her life shushing in the peace. I was enraptured, a magical princess has entered my realm and here she will stay.

I stood for many, many minutes sharing her sleeping world, drinking in her beauty and glorying in my good fortune…

I knock gently on her door and wait for her early morning voice to invite me in.

"Oh, Amy, breakfast in bed. You really shouldn't have done. I haven't had breakfast in bed for years and years."

She reaches her pale, slender arms towards me to take the breakfast tray. I remove the bud vase. "I'll just put this rose here beside you. It is a bit top-heavy and I wouldn't want you to spill it."

"Thank you, Amy. Here sit on the bed. You have only brought one cup. Why don't you bring your drink in here and sit with me?"

I almost skip to the kitchen; I am light-headed with happiness. My dreams are real, she is in my home. She sits now in her bed and we are to breakfast together. The bliss of it all dizzies me as I fill my mug with fresh coffee and tread back up the stairs.

"Amy, about last night."

"Please, Hannah. I apologise. I had made some very silly assumptions and I am truly sorry. Your friendship is so very precious to me. I understand, of course I do, that maybe my feelings for you are not reciprocated. That is fine with me if only it is not a problem for you. More than anything I want us to stay friends. Please now, make my day and tell me we are alright?"

"I admit I was taken aback for a while. I hadn't thought about, well, erm… you know anything other than friendship." A blush creeps up her cheeks and she toys with the butter knife. I am surprised and delighted at her coyness.

"I know, I know." My instinct is to reach to her and take her hand but I hold still. The situation is very delicate. She turns to me.

"Look, I am sorry if I overreacted last night. I value your friendship and, well, as long as it is all in the open and understood that friendship is what it is then everything is fine. Is that alright?"

"That is absolutely wonderful." She smiles with relief and takes a bite of toast. The day is blessed with sunshine, the coffee in my cup is hot and delicious, it is bliss.

"My goodness, Amy, that was a big sigh."

"Ha, yes my dear but a sigh of happiness. I am so happy to have you as a guest and so relieved that we have sorted out our misunderstanding."

"Yes, me too. It was very unfortunate but it's alright now. I was very sorry to hear about your friend, what was her name. Mary?"

The day is spoiled. Just like that the bliss of the moment is shattered, the pleasure tainted and the atmosphere ruined.

"Maria, it was Maria. Please don't talk about it. I don't want you to talk about it."

"Oh, please don't be upset. You know sometimes it is better to talk about the sad things, bring them into the light. Don't you think?"

"No, not in this case, no. You know nothing about it and I don't want you to talk about it. I have to go and sort out the kitchen now. You take your time, enjoy your breakfast, don't rush to come downstairs. Relax, it is Sunday, just relax."

I don't slam the door, I close it carefully, quietly but my nerves jangle, my breath is shortened and my handshakes. Why did she have to do that? I should never have mentioned Maria, what was I thinking?

"I've brought my tray, Amy, thank you so much, that was a lovely treat." She has dressed in jeans and a shirt; her feet are bare and she appears relaxed and at ease. I try to recapture the happiness of before she spoke of Maria but it is there nipping at my heels. She knows now, she knows that there was someone else and it is human nature that she will want to pry and question. It may be better to deal with it now, to lay it to rest so that she can move on and not fuss about it.

"I find it hard to talk about Maria. You do understand, don't you? It is painful for me. I have thought about it, though, and you may be right. It could be that it would do me good to revisit it. Would you mind awfully, it wouldn't be too much of an imposition?"

"No, no of course not. It's what friends do, isn't it? Helping each other, confiding."

"Shall I pour you more coffee?"

"No, no that's fine. Why don't we go and sit on your little patio? It looks to be a lovely morning. Just let me pop back upstairs and I'll join you in a couple of minutes."

She runs back up to the first floor and I step out to wipe the condensation from the table and chairs. The coolness of the breeze is a surprise. From inside the house it seemed that it was a warm morning but there is a chill in the air.

I head for my room and as I pass her door I stop; I will warn her to bring a wrap or a cardigan. I lean towards the wood to tap.

"Yup, getting there. It's slow but there is progress. Speak later." There is a beep.

Who is she calling? Why is she using her mobile in the bedroom? I didn't hear it ring so the call must have been outgoing. A tiny knot of disquiet curls and stretches in my gut.

Chapter 20

Birdsong drips from the trees as the sun warms and opens the few flowers that have made an appearance. A gentle brush of warmth kisses my cheek as we sit in silence on my patio. I detect an air of discomfort. The early camaraderie has dissipated leaving something that I can't pin down. A nervousness has crept between us, probably as a result of the conversation that I feel neither of us really wants to have. I will take control, move things along.

"We didn't live together, Maria and I. We hadn't reached that stage. I had known her a few months and we had only just begun to feel close."

I am aware that I must choose every word in this conversation with great care. I cannot afford to let down my guard for one moment and I must keep it short. "I am not sure I can talk too much about it, you know."

Hannah reaches and touches my arm, she smiles. "I think I understand, only tell me about it if you really want to. I don't want to put you under pressure."

"We met when I was doing part-time work in the college. She wasn't a student of mine, nothing like that. She worked in the administration department. We talked occasionally and of course there was the odd reception where we met and we became friends. We went to the cinema together, that sort of thing."

How much of this can be the truth? I must keep this simple. I wonder now why I have started it. There was no real need, I am confused. She confuses and confounds me. I am struck by a lowering feeling. I wonder if this is the way that I should allow my life to go. I could end it. No, no, the thought is horrible. I have worked so hard to reach this stage I only have to lay this ghost and then we can be happy together. I will hold my nerve. Glancing up I see that she is watching me, her hands are still in her lap, her bag hangs on the back of the chair. Why does her bag hang on the chair? Why does she need her bag, how odd?

"It has always been difficult for me, you know. Relationships. I am older than you my dear and so these things are more awkward for me. I knew from when I was in my teens that there was a difference between my feelings and those of my friends, classmates. We all had crushes on our teachers at school, but for me I think it was different." She coughs, I fear it is with embarrassment. Steeling myself, I continue. I can't look at her now, dreading what I may see in her eyes. Would I see a truth that I don't want to acknowledge? Maybe disgust, as with Maria. This is so hard, I am not sure I can carry it off.

She leans to me again, reaches and squeezes my hand. I believe that she may really want to help. Perhaps in her kindness and her compassion she really does want to help me. Tears leap to my eyes and dribble down my face. I feel ridiculous. What an awful day this is.

"Anyway, I never had boyfriends. I have lived a solitary sort of life. My friends married and so on, but I found it easiest to keep myself involved in my work. University was torture for me, even though my degree is in art, it wasn't as you may think. A popular misconception is that art students are free and easy in their ideas, that they are accepting and open to everything. It's not true, not in the places that I lived and not with the people in my life. Anyway, enough of that. I have never had a close relationship neither with a man or a woman and that's it and all about it."

"But Maria, it was different with Maria – yes?"

Hannah's eyes are kind but her voice has a strange hard edge, or is it imagination on my part?

"At first we were friends, she seemed kind and as though maybe she understood me. I was misled."

"How, how were you misled?" She is pressuring me to tell her things that I need to keep hidden.

"She let me think that maybe there was a chance for something more than friendship. Looking back, I maybe misread the whole thing. I don't know."

"But the accident, you said she had an accident."

"Yes, an accident." My heart thumps my hands shake and I am finding it difficult to take enough air into my lungs. I am dizzy. I can't do this. I must end this now.

"I'm sorry, Hannah, that's all I can say. She is gone, dead and I try not to think about it."

"But what happened, what sort of accident was it, a car, a fall?"

"An accident, that's what it was, a mishap. Let it go, enough."

My head is pounding now, my control is slipping. Why is she insisting on going on? Is it some sort of ghoulish voyeurism? She doesn't need to know this. I thrust to my feet.

"That's enough, Hannah, no more. This isn't helping, let's stop it. I am not feeling too well to be honest."

"Where is she, Amy; where is Maria?" Her voice has hardened, there is a different tone, the kind friend has been overtaken by a harder, firmer character. I glance at her. She is gripping her bag before her, not over her shoulder with the long strap but held awkwardly in her arms. I glance at it and she pulls it closer to her body. There is something wrong. I look back into her eyes, there is guilt there, and there is a glimmer of fear. What is she afraid of, not me? Surely not me?

Chapter 21

I spin away from the garden chair and stagger through the sliding patio doors on legs of India rubber. My stomach churns, I try to find a place of safety. I review what I have told her. Why did I lie, why had I hidden the truth about Maria and I meeting in the supermarket, fabricated the basic facts of the relationship and complicated things beyond all measure? Maria was a nurse, not an administrator. We hadn't met in the college. What can I have been thinking weaving lies and subterfuge to confound and confuse even myself? Trying too hard to be clever and in doing so becoming a fool, an utter fool.

When I had looked into Hannah's eyes they were guarded and suspicious. I was alarmed by the hardness and the coldness there. Could she know and if so, what is the depth of her knowledge? What could she know?

I run through to the downstairs lavatory and reach it just in time before losing control. I vomit the breakfast, the extra coffee, everything in my stomach. I flop empty and shivering onto the tiled floor.

Hannah knocks, "Are you alright, Amy? Do you need anything?"

"Just leave me, would you? Just give me some time."

"Well I don't know, Amy, I think that maybe this is something we should talk about. I mean if you find it so upsetting then maybe it would be better to talk it out."

"Go away, can't you understand me? I don't want to talk about this anymore."

Splashing water on my face I catch a glimpse of my reflection; I am panicked and frantic and it shows clearly on my face.

"Hannah, I think that I am not very well. I am sorry but I think it would be for the best if you left. I can call you tomorrow but really I need to be alone just now."

"Oh, not at all, Amy, I can't leave now. Come on out and let me take care of all this. I want to be your friend, Amy, I thought we cared for each other. Come out now and let's talk it all through."

Her words are strange, her tone is cold and measured – at odds with the words. She sounds not at all the concerned friend but more a bystander, a stranger. A cold chill sweeps through me, there is something here that is very, very wrong.

She knows, doesn't she? By some strange power she knows. I sink to the floor, my back against the wall. I don't understand what has happened, my thoughts spiral and spin and I can't hold them. I see the broken, bloody body that had once been Maria, I see the blood-stained carpet and the darkened woodland. I see again the mound of earth and smell the damp undergrowth and I am sure now that somehow Hannah knows.

All of a sudden I am calm, my heart stops the frantic tap dance and my brain clears. There is no way to fathom how she knows and there is no way to understand why it matters to her, but this person has found my secret, has somehow divined the most damning truth, and now I must act.

Chapter 22

Straightening my back and squaring my shoulders I rub with the towel until my face looks almost normal and the ruin is obliterated. I call out through the door.

"Hannah, Hannah. Wait just a moment, I'm sorry. I'm alright really. Just give me another moment to gather my wits. Hold on."

"Oh, are you sure? Shall I go through to the sitting room? I'll wait in there for you. I'll wait until you're ready."

"Yes, would you? That'll be fine. I'll be there just now."

I open the cloakroom door and step into the hall. Back in the sitting room she is waiting perched on the edge of the easy chair near the window. She looks edgy and over excited. Her face is flushed and her eyes sparkle. In spite of the turmoil of the last hour I am again overwhelmed by her beauty. There is something wrong, though. My angel has a dark worm in her soul. I don't know what it is, I can't fathom her thinking. Why is she so preoccupied with my past relationship? We had already agreed that our friendship would be simply that, and so what difference does any of it make to her?

Whatever the cause there is too much risk here and I am going to be forced to act in some way. I have spent the last years keeping myself to myself. I have worked at home all those lonely hours and carefully managed my social engagements. There has been so much effort to avoid suspicion forming anywhere. I have never allowed anyone to get close and have not let myself become involved with much. In fact, my life has been terribly restricted, and I am not willing to allow all that to have been in vain.

The few people I still see from the time of Maria believe my version of events. I explained that she simply left for a better job. Some of them had understood how strong my feelings had been, they were discreet and kind. Nothing was ever said, I allowed no prying questions, I kept relationships cool and maintained a distance. It has suited my purposes perfectly. Now, though, it is all at risk and I have no option but to take steps to protect myself. A plan is forming and even as I walk into the room and pin a smile on my face, my mind races with the scheme.

"My dear." I cross to the window and kneel before her, taking her hand in mine. It is shaking, why is that? "I am so very sorry for all of this dreadful hysteria. I am embarrassed and would turn back time if I was able. I have spoilt our lovely day and feel so sad about that. I don't often allow myself to think about Maria, I miss her very much, you see. I find it all very painful. You can understand that can't you?"

"Oh yes, of course. I see that I shouldn't have pushed so hard. I was trying to help, really I was." She draws her hand away and places it back on the top of the leather bag. Why is she still carting that thing about? I don't remember this obsession before. All morning she has had this clumsy black shoulder bag with her.

"Let me take that and put it away in the hall cupboard for you."

She clutches it tightly and her knuckles whiten against the skin of her hands. "No, no it's fine I'll just keep it with me. I like to have it near, my tissues are in it you know, things I may need."

I turn and look pointedly at the box of tissues on the side table and she blushes. My nerves are on full alert, they tingle and I still can't pin down the reasons.

"I've been thinking about it all, my dear, and I wonder if you really can help me with this."

A smile curls her lips but doesn't reach her eyes. Subterfuge and dissembling, I sense it.

"Of course, of course just tell me what you want me to do."

"Well, only if you want to; if you feel you can do it. I wondered if you would come with me and visit her grave." Her eyes flick to the side as her fingers twitch against the leather of the bag on her lap.

"Oh, oh yes of course. Yes, certainly I will do that. Do you want to do it now today?"

"Well, I think that the last hours have put me into a strange place and I really do think that it would be a good time. Do you think that we could? Shall we take your car? I can tell you where to go."

"Is she not in the cemetery then?"

"The cemetery, no, no – not the town one. Such a horrid place down there near the shops, no she is somewhere much nicer."

"Amy."

"Mmm, what is it my dear?"

"You didn't tell me how she died, what sort of accident was it?"

"Ah yes. It was a domestic accident I'm afraid. Yes, a horrible accident in the home."

"A fall?"

"Mmmm, a fall. She fell. Let me sort myself out, I will change and then off we go. No rush of course but do you think that you might want to pack your things, get them together? It is getting late and it will be quite dark by the time we come back and you'll be ready to go home."

"Pack my things… oh, well, yes of course. If that's what you want."

"Well to be perfectly honest I am feeling drained and I would rather like a quiet evening, I think it would be good for me to be alone. We will visit Maria and then you can drop me off. Will that be alright do you think?"

"Yes, yes I'll go and sort out the bedroom."

There is a toolbox in the hall cupboard, I take a hammer and a small trowel. It is not ideal but I have to be able to make this look innocent.

"Ready, Amy, I'll put the things in my car."

"Yes, I'm coming." Joining her on the driveway I see her eyes flick to the large holdall I have with me.

"I hope it's alright but it occurred to me that maybe the grave will need tidying. I have a couple of gardening tools. Not a problem is it?"

"No, no that's fine. Do you want to put them in the boot?"

"Excellent. Now then, off we go. Take the road up towards the Heath. Let me put that big bag of yours on the floor here."

"Okay, careful, it doesn't have a clasp. Don't tip it. The Heath did you say? Up to the Heath."

We drive through my gate. For the second time in such a few days I am heading back to the woods. My throat is dry and my hands quiver and shake at what I am about to do.

Chapter 23

The beautiful sunny start to the day is lost, lowering skies are painted with shades of misery colouring through to black. There is the feel of rain in the air. And my soul is filled with the melancholy of the clouds.

As we near the Heath I notice that the few people around are heading towards the town. The threatening weather is actually on my side. The woods will be deserted.

The great car pulls into the parking space, little more than a flattened area of earth it serves because the Heath is mostly visited by dog walkers and kite flyers but not many car drivers. Children on bikes screech and laugh here and lovers stroll in the evenings.

We clamber down. "Where are we going, Amy? I didn't know there was a cemetery here."

"No, it is one of those new environmentally sympathetic ones. No markings and not many people know about it. Only those of us who have been to a burial really know about it."

She looks unsure but shrugs and turns to retrieve the leather bag which I had stowed in the footwell.

"You don't need to bring that really. It's not far."

"Oh, I know, but it is such a habit. Us women and our bags, eh." She smiles at me.

There is falseness about her. The air crackles with tension, or is it my heightened tension? I am afraid.

I am overwhelmed and turn to hide the swell of tears in my eyes. From here I can see the town laid out before me. With the early darkness there are lights popping into the gloom. Ribbons of brightness are drawn around the streets and in the distance there is a dark sheet of rain reaching down from the heavens. It is quite lovely in a wild way, nature unkempt and untamed as it must be. My life has become that now, fate or kismet has taken control and I am simply a tool or more properly a weapon acting for self-preservation.

I am empty, my heart is a great weight in my chest and my head pounds. I reach into the boot of the car and retrieve the tools. "Come along, my dear, let's get this done before the rain comes." As I turn, I notice that the cars are now switching on their headlights and down amongst the houses I see blue sparkles, an ambulance or the fire brigade? At any rate there is someone else in trouble today. Maybe another like myself whose life will be changed irrevocably by the events of a day that began with sunshine.

I turn to trek across the bare earth to the trees. She follows slowly, glancing back a couple of times, the woods do not look welcoming. The shades and shadows are blackened against new leaves that are unnaturally green in the stormy light.

We follow the casual route, the desire path and tread carefully over exposed roots ducking and bending to avoid the branches. She stumbles and I reach out to steady her and acknowledge her weak smile. She is also afraid. The fear shakes her hands and flits into her eyes. Her pale skin is yet paler, corpse like. I think that there are tears on her lashes, why should she cry? Does she suspect or is it simply tension reflected by the very air between us? No matter, the die is cast and I tread firmly over the uneven ground heading for the clearing and the great pine tree.

Chapter 24

The rain has reached us. There has not been enough yet to cause the trees to drip into the woods but the moisture chills our faces and dampens our clothes.

"Is it far? I wonder if we should turn back. We don't have raincoats on."

"Not long now, Hannah, not long. Can you walk in front, do you think? Just follow the path. You are more surefooted than I am, I think."

"Okay if you like. Straight on?"

"Yes, that's right, just follow this path. I'll tell you when to turn."

My voice catches in my throat as the emotion threatens to overwhelm me. I wonder if I can do this. The last time it was sudden, an explosion of fury and violence, and the result was Maria bloody and broken on my carpet. This is so different, contrived and preconceived. Is this what I am now, have I truly become a monster? Dizziness overcomes me again.

The passion is too much for my mental state. I lean against a damp trunk for a moment as she picks her way before me along the dark path.

As I stare at her narrow back and the blonde hair flat with moisture, lying on her shoulders in tails and strands, I have to remind myself what I am about. She is suspicious, she has moved on from interested to questioning and suspicion. The risk to my survival is too great. I renew my grip on the rain slick handle of my holdall and quietly undo the zipper. Groping in the dark I find the handle of the hammer. I can barely breathe, reality is suspended, a few more moments to walk closer. I am now within reach; she turns to me.

"This is silly, isn't it? Surely we can do this when the rain goes off."

I look into her eyes and see a flicker of fear, her lips part and she freezes like a wild thing caught in the headlights of a truck. Silence has descended, my ears have ceased to hear. My brain is shutting out the dreadful moments, closing off like a child in the darkness. Now I am animal, now I am fighting for survival. She turns again.

"Amy, what's wrong? Amy, Amy."

As I watch she scrabbles in her black bag, glancing down and then back. Struggling with the handles and the belongings inside, she is starting to panic. She has divined my intent, I must be humane. I must finish this quickly, it should be like dispatching a fish, no time for terror. She has dropped the damned bag and the contents have spilled onto the forest floor. She falls to her knees scrabbling amongst the dirt and detritus. She is sobbing now, frantic and panicked. She snatches at a dark shape in the heap of belongings amongst the tree roots. She pushes backwards, crawling crablike along the path.

I take short swift steps. My arm is half raised now; the hammer head shines in the feeble glow of the rain-washed moon. She looks up at me from her crouched position. There are tears running down her cheeks but she has stopped sobbing and raises her hands in front of her body. Both hands stretch towards me but not in defence, is it in supplication? She holds the dark object from her bag as if she is offering it to me. What can it be, what is that? I take two more steps towards her bending now but with the hammer still held high. I am ready to strike but what is this thing in her hand, what is she trying to give me?

"Amy Jobson, I arrest you for the murder of Maria Portious. You are not obliged…"

"No. What is this? No." Leaping forward I hear an animal screech and realize that it comes from my mouth, from my soul. My hand descends, bringing the glob of steel slicing through the gloom and the world explodes with a violent flash of light. My ears are forced back to function by the thunder to be immediately muffled by a second deafness as they react to the noise. An earthquake throws me from my feet and I crash back against a tree trunk. She has regained her feet and runs towards me.

The air is filled with light and sound. Flashing blue fills my eyes, filtered through the branches, howling creatures surround me. The noise is all consuming, there is a fire in my leg, which refuses to function. She stands above me. How is it that I am here on the damp earth? Shapes continue to move through the trees; there is shouting and wavering torchlights.

"Hannah, Hannah."

"Over here, Sarge, down here. Call an ambulance, we need an ambulance."

She kneels over me. Her hair falls forward in a damp curtain as she leans towards me. "Don't try to move, Amy; keep as still as you can. You'll be alright. An ambulance is coming."

"Hannah, I don't understand. What has happened?"

"There will be time, Amy, I can explain later. Let's get you to the hospital first." She turns to call out to the gathering figures. "Sarge, she's losing a lot of blood here."

I feel her fingers groping at the top of my leg and the pressure as she tries to stem the flow of blood. It is darker now, the moon has gone and the pain is dissipating. The figures stand amongst the trees, radios crackle and the torches shine their unforgiving beams towards us.

Chapter 25

"Stay with me, Amy. Look at me." Hannah's voice is in my ears but she is distant and insubstantial. I try to concentrate. I gaze at her lovely face muddied now and with tears and rain streaming across her cheeks. I try to squeeze her hand but I have no strength. I don't feel much at all. It is pleasant like a warm bath, floating at ease.

"Who are you, Hummingbird? What is this?" She leans closer in the gloom. The other figures loiter on the periphery of our world mumbling and shuffling. "What has this been? Has it not been real at all?"

"Amy, don't worry about all that now. Tell me, Amy, where is Maria? Where is her body?"

"Her body?" Darkness descends momentarily showing me peace but I am dragged back. Hannah is shaking me.

"Amy, don't you do that, stay with me now. Tell me where she is, Amy. It's all you can do now to put this right."

"Is that all there is for you, Hannah? All you care about is Maria? What about me, don't I matter? Has our friendship meant nothing?"

"I'm sorry, I was doing my job that's all, let me finish it, Amy. Tell me where she is."

"Your job! That is what this has been to you, just a job?"

"No never just a job, I believe in justice, Amy. So much of my recent life has been taken up with you and what you did. Months of planning and preparing."

"Watching me, baiting your trap and pulling me in. How clever you must have felt, you and your compatriots. How you must have laughed at me." I feel wetness on my cheeks now as useless tears trickle across to run under my ears and seep into the earth on the forest floor.

"Amy, we needed to find her, needed her body. People can't just disappear, Maria was missed. The ones who loved her missed her and those same people need to have closure. Tell me now where she is and do the right thing. We can take care of you, Amy, the ambulance is coming for you. Help me now, let me take Maria back to her family and then we can finish this."

"I loved her, I did and I loved you, Hannah. Did you know that I loved you?"

"I know you loved her and I don't think you meant to hurt her, so this is a chance to put it right. Come on, Amy, if you loved her let us take her away from this dark place."

I can see her face ruined by the night and I hear the noise of the ambulance screaming through the storm. I am betrayed and my heart is shredded. There was no truth to our friendship, never any hope for love to grow and this beautiful creature was no more than a filthy sham. There is nothing to hold me here and I feel my spirit called away and I find no reason to fight. I will take one last look and scorch the image of her face on my retina. I will close my eyes now, it is too hard to hold them open. I hear her still screeching at me like a harridan, "Stay with me, Amy, don't you do this. Stay with me."

Ah, Hannah, my pretty Hummingbird, how can I stay with you when you never really existed at all? The darkness deepens and I shan't fight it any more. Here is Maria. She is here in the woods and she beckons.

PART TWO

Chapter 26

"Amy, Amy, oh Christ." Her limp body wobbles grotesquely as I shake her shoulders. I know I'm crying, I can't cry, I mustn't be weak, not now. My heart is pounding against my chest wall and blood is throbbing in my throat and head. I believe I have already acknowledged on some level that my life is changed forever. The sounds around me are dulled, I feel in some strange way both a part of it, everything extremely clear and vivid, but at the same time totally divorced from reality. The biggest thing, the only thing that is getting through is the fact that I have probably killed another human being.

She was a murderer, dreadfully flawed and undoubtedly the nearest thing that I had ever yet seen to real evil. Her self-interest and total self-absorption had expunged many of the emotions that make us human. At this moment though, kneeling amongst the leaf mould in the flickering shards of light from the emergency vehicles, all I see is a woman that I had known, lying broken amongst the rain spattered pools of blood around my knees. My hands are black with the slippery gore where I tried to stem the flow from her wound. I think she is dead and there is nothing I can do.

She spoke a name before her eyes closed. Maria. Was that who she saw in that moment? Or was that who she wanted to be with her then? She had trusted me, she told me that she loved me and I had known that. What I, what we, have done is right and legal and approved and it has been planned for an age, but with a different ending. Right now, down amongst the tree roots the only real thing is the knowledge that I may have taken a life.

"Hannah, come out from there, Hannah. Let the medics in, move yourself!" Reality collides with my fugue, smashing it aside. Rough hands drag me backwards through the mud and the rain. Sergeant Collins spins me towards him, his face looming into my vision. "Hannah, come on get a grip. Hannah, where's the weapon? Your gun? We need your gun. Come on get it together." The night and the sounds and the cold assault me and I realise that I am shaking, sodden hair trails in rat's tails across my face and I am dripping with cold wet rain.

"Right, yeah, right. Okay, yeah, the weapon. I'm here, Sarge. I'm okay, it's okay." I have to grab at the soggy strands of the wig pulling them away from my eyes but in the end the only thing that I can do is to drag it fully away from my head. Underneath the covering my own hair is dryer and at least it's short and out of my face. Almost like magic, with the wig goes the panic and loss of control. I am back in charge, a tough police officer, weapon trained, undercover, but am I also now forever a killer? The bile rises in my throat and I run tripping on the roots and rubble as far as I can from the scene. If I had vomited there, I would've contaminated the area but more than that the team would have seen me, and I'm not having that.

Chapter 27

Leaning against the bark of an old chestnut tree, I gulp in great mouthfuls of cold, damp air. My eyes stream and bile has scorched my throat but the vomiting seems to have stopped. I hate being sick, have done since I was a kid. A frantic scrabble in my jacket comes up with a couple of old tickets but no tissues and no handkerchief; at times like this I have to acknowledge that my mum did know best. She would have had a neat little triangle of freshly laundered linen, probably with a tiny embroidered daisy in the corner. A great sob throws itself from my throat and for a moment, I really want my mum. *Christ, Hannah, get yourself together, you wuss.*

My handbag is back in the middle of the post-shooting frenzy, lying in the mud and blood. It's probably ruined anyway but all I need now is something to wipe my eyes and mouth. I drag the ends of my sleeves down but they're soaked with

Amy's blood and simply smear dark marks onto my palms. I unzip my jacket and drag the sweater hem free, tugging it upwards with both hands. The cold slaps at my bare midriff and as I rub with the polyester to clear my eyes, I can only hope I'm not just smearing blood, mud and vomit all over my face. What a wreck.

A great cleansing breath draws damp air into my lungs as I turn to trudge back to the noise, the lights and vehicles, which have turned what was in fact a scene of horror into something approaching a fairground. The ambulance is turning into the main road, blue lights flash from the roof but there is no siren and the silence speaks volumes. Is she to be Brought In Dead, B.I.D?

As I stumble nearer to the path a uniformed officer passes me on his way between the trees with tape, winding it round the trunks. Trimming the scene with baleful bunting.

"Hannah, over here." Sergeant Collins is holding me with a grip around my upper arm. "We've got your gun and your bag; we're looking for the spent cases and we've got her bag and the bloody great hammer. I think we should go back now and you can make your statement in the warm. Are you okay? Well, you'll have to be, there'll be questions to answer; you know that, don't you?"

I manage a nod.

"Right, go with Mike and Sammy, we're pretty well sorted here. There're more officers on the way to help to secure the area and the SOCO team are already parking up down there." He points back up the pathway to where I had parked the car. "We'll leave your car there for now."

"Okay." I think that my voice sounds strong and I am standing firm and steady. With a quick squeeze of my shoulders, which changes into a slight push in the direction he wants me to go, he dismisses me.

* * *

Back at the office I cradle a mug of coffee. The lights, the desks and computers, the windows, doors, the horrible grey carpet tiles – they're all so familiar. They feel like home, yet I'm changed so very completely from the person I was when I had been here last. Only a week ago I'd paid a quick clandestine visit, knowing that Amy was safe at the theatre, a show I had opted out of – Shakespeare is beyond me. I had popped in to update the team on progress, which at that time had been slow. Now, it's over and being over is only the beginning. There will be an investigation into the shooting. I'm sure that I'm in the clear, aren't I? She came at me with a hammer, killing in her eyes and I had shouted a warning. I run it through in my mind over and over, it was self-defence, my life had been in imminent danger and I had fired because I had no other choice but, my God, what a mess it's left.

This isn't the conclusion that we had planned. I had been supposed to persuade her to take me to where she had buried Maria's body and then make a nice clean arrest. Body, murderer, arrest – job done. Instead of that, I've let everyone down, and we still don't have Maria's body. There's nobody to see as I lay my head on the desk for a moment and try to still the clamour in my brain.

Chapter 28

The hot water sluices down through my hair, flushing over my shoulders and pooling around my feet where the old plumbing just can't cope with the flow. It's wonderful. My bathroom glints and shines, clean tiles, pretty bottles and tubes, and my glass holding a toothbrush and razor all sparkling under the spotlights in the ceiling. I rest my head against the shower screen and watch through the waterfall as the scene before me ripples and blurs. I am trapped by the warmth and the water. At first the deluge ran muddy pink, and bile filled my throat again as I watched the remnants of Amy's blood flow away.

Now the pool is clean, but I still feel the ghost of the sticky mess on my face, in my hair and between my fingers. I've been bloodied before, of course I have, but this is different. This is blood that I've drawn; I tried to stop the flow even as I was kneeling in it, burying my hands in it and when I scrambled away it spread over my arms and soaked into my clothes.

We've got showers at the police station but I waited until I could tear off my pants and top and underwear and fling them into the waste bin. I wanted to be alone to have no time constraints and no need to speak to anyone afterwards. I needed this, this chance to sink into the warmth and lose myself in the perfume and the purity.

I've made my statement, short and factual and I signed the paper, but I'm not kidding myself, tomorrow it'll all start up again. I know I'll be interviewed, questioned and consulted. An appointment will probably already have been made with the psychologist and the doctor. No doubt I'll be called before the assistant chief constable. I know there'll be a mixture of concern about my welfare and worry about how the investigation will progress. We must be shown to be totally in the right, the fact that she had been a killer is not enough to prove my innocence – not really relevant, in an odd way. The weeks and months of planning will need to be explained, the undercover operation will have to be justified and the final dreadful outcome is going to be pulled apart. Decisions will be made about all of it.

Countless hours, well, in truth counted hours – counted recorded and logged. Weeks in the planning. Watching her day by day until her regular routines were established. The unmissable trip to the post office and the stop-off at Costa each Tuesday without fail. The undercover work proper, a farce at times, trying to be in the right place at the right time. The queue in the paper shop, the same table at the same time as near as possible in the coffee shop. The shawl, the cursed shawl left for her to grab and steal and then return. She danced to our tune, no mistake, and we thought we were so very clever. It all panned out so very well until the final act when the luck ran out in grand style and we still don't know where the body is.

I am bone weary, overwhelmed, exhausted and I have to grab for the wash basin as I stagger out of the tub and try to reach my towel. Suddenly my eyes will barely stay open. I give my hair a quick rub. Thank heavens it's short, not trailing round my face and shoulders like the blasted wig. It's still a bit damp but it'll have to do. I need my bed. I take a quick stop in the kitchen for a mug of milk, zapped in the microwave and cheered with a splash of brandy.

Oh, the bliss of my mattress and the duvet, I drag it up over my shoulders, I am shivering again now but I'm not cold; it's reaction, shock. I am going into the comfort of the dark, I flick off all the lights. I will leave the tiny one on the bedside cabinet lit in case I wake in the night. I'll clear my mind, wipe it all away. Just for now, for the next few hours I need to blank it all out and become what I was before.

Chapter 29

I've no idea how long I've slept. I've no idea how long the doorbell's been ringing but it dragged me back through the dark dreams to reality. I stagger down the hall. Peering into the spy hole all I see is a vague silhouette, the back of a head and shoulders. The lights in the hallway are programmed to dim automatically after midnight and a glance at my watch confirms that it's nearly two in the morning.

"Hello, who is it? Hello." There's no answer and the figure hardly moves – just a mere twitch. I've no idea who this is but after the events of yesterday it could be anyone. I suppose it could be a representative of the Police Federation – unlikely at this hour. The psychologists, maybe, one of the lads? It's an odd time but it's possible – a quick check to see that I'm okay on my own. There is the other possibility I suppose, heaven forbid but it could be a reporter who's found me in spite of all the precautions we've taken.

"Hello, who the hell is it? I'm not opening this door unless you tell me who it is. Where are you from?"

"Open the door, Hannah, I'm cold out here."

The world tips and skews and my mind reels as reality battles to reassert control against disbelief.

"Amy?" I hear the whisper slither from my throat. "No, come on. No." The figure rotates slowly in the gloom and the familiar face looms, slightly distorted into the fisheye lens.

"Let me in, Hannah. Please."

I can't make my fingers work; they're quivering and struggling with the security chain. The metal rattles and clinks, the chain slips and clatters against the wood of the door frame. I hear a gasping loud in the pre-dawn quiet. It's me panting with shock and fear. I am outside myself. I hear myself muttering trying to deny the truth of my own eyes. "Oh no, it can't be. No. Come on."

The chain gives and I drag at the handle throwing back the door and stepping into the frame. My head is shaking in denial, and I can't stop the trembling, but there she is in the hallway. She is still dressed in the same clothes and the blood has dried leaving dark stiffened patches on the fabric. There are splashes of blood on her legs and her grey hair is dark and clinging around her face clotted with mud.

"No, it isn't, it can't be. Amy?"

She doesn't speak, she doesn't move. Her eyes sparkle in the light of the hallway and a timid smile plays about her lips. Her head is tipped to one side as she watches me retreat against the wall. I know my hand is over my mouth because I have bitten the side of it. I feel hot tears flowing across my cheeks. I know this can't be.

"What do you want? Why aren't you dead? You're dead. I thought you were dead."

Still she doesn't speak, standing mute in the hallway, mute and immobile until, after what seems an age, she raises a hand towards me. "Come on, my dear. Come with me, you wanted to find her, come on let me take you to her now."

The wall I'm leaning against is the only real thing in the world.

"I thought you were dead; I saw them take you away. How can you be here?" As I speak, I realise that what I am saying isn't strictly true. I had been dragged off by the Sergeant and the demands of my nauseated body had scurried me away to puke into the undergrowth. I had watched the ambulance turn into the road and scorch off in the direction of the hospital. I had never seen her pronounced dead, I had never seen the body lying on a slab in the morgue, never seen her in a shroud.

If she's not dead that means that I'm not a killer. Hope blooms.

"My coat. I have to get my coat." She stands with her hands by her sides, her head tilted; waiting in that quiet way that she always had. I dash through to the hall cupboard and throw on a coat over my pyjamas. I drag on my wellies and run back to the door. I tumble out onto the landing to find that she's already heading for the stairs. I hurry to catch up, my heart in my throat, my legs threatening to let me down. The distance between us is immense.

"Wait, wait for me, Amy; wait, I can't keep up." She's getting away, further and further, the wellies I've dragged on aren't mine, they're too big. My feet are slipping and sliding and my legs are losing their strength as I stagger towards the stairs. "Amy, Amy wait." I am running through treacle, something is holding me back, the world has slowed.

"AMY!"

The duvet is wrapped around my legs, the dim light from the streetlamp glints on my bedroom mirror as the nightmare that was Amy dissolves into the darkness.

Chapter 30

I crawl into the shower, feeling like death warmed over. After the dream, nightmare, whatever you want to call it, I tossed and turned until the darkness leeched into grey dawn.

I have had many sleepless nights since joining the police – it goes with the territory. It usually leaves me with a feeling of frustration and disappointment. When the dawn unfolds and the events we have been hoping for haven't happened, or things other than expected have gone down, then the dissatisfaction is very lowering. Today, though, I couldn't wait for the light. I wanted a new day. I need to be busy and to start to wind things up and move on.

I force down some toast and coffee, standing at the kitchen counter. I tidy the bed, lock up and clatter down the stairs and out to the parking area. For a minute I'm confused when I can't find my car, and then I remember that it's been impounded. This ongoing review will impact my every day for a little while yet. I plip the key and cross the drive to the pool car that I'm assigned.

The office is quiet. It's early, just after seven, so I don't have to walk through the workspace under the gaze of my colleagues. Some of them would be sympathetic and understanding. They would just carry on with their own work and leave me be. There will be some, though, who will want to know all about the shooting, the woods, the whole damn thing and I just can't face them yet. Not today. Even the force has its share of ghouls.

I had wondered myself what it would feel like. When I trained to use weapons, I knew on some sort of level that the reason I was doing it would be that I may have to shoot at someone one day. I had talked to people who had experience of it. I had read reports and I had tried to imagine what it would be like. But there is no way that you can imagine it. It isn't playacting, it isn't television, it isn't a video game. Yesterday showed me that it's real, very real, and it hits you deep inside.

I have to get past it, to put it away in its box and to move on, but every time I close my eyes, I see her. Lying in the mud, the rain soaking into her grey hair as the blood washes around us and she gives me one last look before closing her eyes. The real world is on a different level to me, other people are in a different zone.

I will not let this define me, I was acting in the line of duty and self-defence. She was evil, she was a murderer and she meant me harm.

She was Amy, she loved me.

I have failed. We still don't have Maria's body, I feel moisture on the back of my hand and stare at it, bemused for a while. It's the tears dripping from my eyes. I dash them away and drag some paperwork towards me. This will not get to me.

Chapter 31

"Hannah, hey Hannah. Come up here."

In all the time that I've spent in this house I never did go up to the third floor. I had never thought about it apart from registering that it existed. Now Sergeant Collins is yelling down the stairs and I have to go up there.

It feels weird being here, it really does.

The last time I was here was with Amy. She was hysterical and frightening. We had reached the end game as far as I was concerned. I had known that if she didn't take me to Maria's grave right then I had probably blown it and we were never going to get any further. We'd gone out to my car. She was carting a great bag with her and she told me that it was stuff to tidy up the grave in a natural burial site. You don't do that; it's the whole point isn't it? There is no grave. It was such a tense time I hadn't seen the contradiction. Even if I had, it wouldn't have mattered. I had already decided at that point that I had to go with her and see it through.

I hadn't realised that she was way ahead of me. She'd even planned enough to bring the spade ready to bury my body. A shiver ripples through me as I think of it and I force myself to start climbing the stairs up towards the raised voice and the clumping footsteps on the ceiling. I'm tough, I can do this. "Bloody hell, Hannah, are you comin'?"

"Yeah."

"Look at this." As I push through the door Bob Collin's hand sweeps a wide arc around the space tucked away in the roof of the old house.

"Jesus." I'm standing in a faithful copy of the office that we had mocked up in town. It had been a simple, sparse set up because of time and financial constraints but it had been enough to convince Amy. Not only that, she reproduced it exactly in the top of her own home.

"What the hell is this for?" But I know, let's face it, if anyone would know it should be me. I'm the one who got close to her, I'm the one who effectively knitted the web that trapped her. We stare at each other as the thoughts and ideas trip and tumble.

"She was going to have you here, wasn't she?"

I just nod at Bob.

"Well, it looks that way. Do you think she intended to lock me up? Surely not, she wasn't that mad, was she?"

"She was a mad bitch, no doubt about it, but this… Think of how much this cost. Think of the effort and organisation needed to get it done so quickly. How did she remember what it looked like?"

I riffle through piles of printouts on one of the shelves.

"Well, this explains it." I hold out sheets and sheets of screen grabs showing the pictures we had posted on the fake website. Office interior shots, staged interviews for magazines and fake advertising blurb. "She's used these and what she remembered and my god she got it very nearly perfect."

"Well, it didn't do her any good in the end and it didn't do you any harm. I'll get it photographed and packed up. Carry on with what you were doing."

It hadn't done me any harm. No, not until just now. Nausea builds as I clomp back down the narrow flight of stairs. The threat lingering in that space has chilled me. *Push it back, Hannah, push it away.*

I enter the back bedroom where I'd slept as her guest. This room had freaked me out when I'd first seen it. There'd been bottles of the perfume I was using and a cream shawl like the one that I had used to get Amy to contact me. There'd been a nightdress like the ones I usually wear; how the hell did she get the exact same one? If I had realised then the depth of the obsession, I'm not sure I would have ever have risked the trip in the car.

Again, my thoughts are whirling. If I'd known about this and chickened out, I wouldn't have shot her. We would still have a chance of finding Maria. I flop into the chair and lower my head into my hands. I am chilled by a sheen of sticky sweat; I can feel my heart pumping away and for a moment reality retreats and takes me to a dark place where I float and spin.

"Are you okay, Hannah?" A strong hand is rocking my shoulder, "Hey, come on, are you okay?" I look up into Bob Collin's worried blue eyes. "Have you been to see the psychologist yet?"

I shake my reeling head and nausea threatens again.

"Well do it today. You look like shit. Come on let's go and get a cuppa. You really are going to have to get this sorted, Hannah. You're no good to me like this." He smiles as he speaks but there is deep concern behind his look and a trace of impatience. I am letting him down; this is wimpy behaviour and there's no room for it. I push myself up and follow him out of the house.

Chapter 32

The rain is torrential, I can't see. I'm soaked to the skin and I don't know where this is. Roots and weeds tangle around my ankles and legs; they tear and tug, causing me to stumble and fall. There's mud everywhere, cold and cloying.

I'm sobbing, hiccupping with it, and gulping and gasping but I can't stop. Snot has trickled from my nose and as I swipe at it with my sticky fingers the slimy mess smears across my cheek.

If only I could see to get some bearings. If I could stand steady and walk normally and just understand what was happening to me.

I crash forward half crouching to avoid the slapping overhead branches that reach and claw at my eyes and head. "Help me, oh God, where am I? Is there anyone there? Please help me."

Staggering blindly, reaching into the gloom my hand finds a slippery tape and clutches it. Bending to see, my eyes peering through the dimness find only light and dark. A slick pliable hardness sliding between my fingers cutting at my palms. Dragging it upwards I squint through the gloom – there is lettering. Police.

With a great mental crack, I am back in my own reality. I am here, here in the woods. How did I get here? Why? Shock throws me onto my behind to plop down amongst the soaked grass and the puddles. How in the name of all that's holy did I get here?

I'm wearing no coat and the shivering is uncontrollable now. I know I'm grinding my fingernails into my palms, I can't unclench them. Is this another bloody dream? Pain tingles in the palms of my hands. Can you feel pain in a dream? I think not.

The world is a vicious, hostile place and I am a cowering, feeble creature. Curling against the trunk of a great tree I hide my face down in my knees. Crying out loud now. "Help me, help me."

Now I am located and know this place, I have been here before. Amy's blood has flowed into this grass. Her body lay amongst these roots. I must get away.

Leaping to my feet I run and stagger and fall and drag myself up again and onwards. My feet find the path and I stand straighter now on the more solid ground. Cold rain is beating against my face and mixing with salt tears. With a deep breath and a massive effort, I stop and calm myself and take my bearings.

This is the woods on the hill. I am filthy, hardly dressed and soaked to the skin and have no idea at all how I came to be here.

I can't stop sobbing, like the wimp that I'm going to become if I don't deal with this. But I've got more control now as I turn towards the lights of the town glowing down below. I head for the thinner line of trees and where the car park should be. Will my car be there? I don't know. I am completely unconnected with anything that may have brought me here and can't remember what happened.

My name is Hannah. I am a policewoman. I remember Amy, I remember I shot her. Bill Collins sent me home from work early because he was worried about me after the visit to Amy's house.

If I close my eyes, I see my flat earlier today. I can remember driving into the car park and unlocking the front door. After that there is nothing. Blankness from the moment I walked into my home in the daylight. Now it is deep night and I have to get back.

The car is in the car park, not the great black four-wheel drive but the small pool car. The door is unlocked and the key is in the ignition. The key slides between my wet fingers and I have to dry them shivering and quaking on a tissue from the box on the dashboard. The engine fires and the lights illuminate the calm, ordinary, rainy night.

I drive home shivering and gasping in a half daze through midnight streets. They are deserted except for the few late workers and the homeless and the scurrying stragglers. I turn into my driveway. The key to my front door is on the same ring as my car key and I slam the door behind me.

Tearing off my clothes I step into the steaming shower and slide to the floor with the hot water beating on my head. My God, what is happening to me? Am I losing my mind?

Chapter 33

I have started lying. I didn't intend to but it grew from subterfuge. I wasn't all that keen to see the psychologist right from the start. Not many people want to "open up" but it has been proven to be valuable. When there has been an incident that could be traumatic it's now become part of the procedure.

I was on edge and nervy, thinking about the appointment. Last night was horrible. Waking in the pouring rain amongst the trees was terrifying and I am still absolutely thrown by it. It was impossible for me to miss work and doubly impossible for me to miss the appointment with Mrs Harker.

Bill Collins was his usual self when I arrived at work. "Christ, Hannah, you look bloody terrible," was his greeting and I knew he was right.

"Think I could be coming down with a bug." I walked on past him concentrating on the set of my shoulders and the spring in my step. The tears were a moment away. *There is no room for this, this is not the way that I want to behave and this is not the way that I want to feel. I have to get myself together.* The thoughts tumbled as I made my way to the psychologist's office. *Actually, it could be that I do need to unload. Maybe it could do some good and help to get me back on track.*

She wears a skirt and blouse and a soft cardigan. The office is warm and she's looking relaxed in a low chair when I slide through the door.

"Hi there, Hannah. Is it okay if I call you Hannah?"

I nod and sit on the chair opposite to her.

"Okay, bit of a formality really." She smiles at me, "Of course that's not to say that you shouldn't take the whole thing seriously. You have been through a potentially life-changing situation and if you have any concerns at all I am here to try and help. What we say here is confidential but I will make a report. That will simply be my opinion on whether or not you need more support and your fitness for full duties. Okay?"

I manage another smile; it feels strained and forced but she doesn't seem to notice. I carefully wipe my sweating palms on my trousers as she bends to pour herself a drink.

"Water?" She slides a glass towards me.

"So, I have seen a report of what happened. You had your copy?" Her eyes flick to my face for a moment and she registers my nod. Leaning back against the padding she crosses her hands loosely on her lap. "First of all, is there anything that is particularly bothering you? Since the incident particularly, of course, but I am here to listen to any concerns you may have."

The silence stretches between us and I struggle with the decision about how much I should say.

"What sort of thing do you mean?" Feeble, feeble. Playing for time and she is sure to know.

"Well, do you think that you are dealing with the trauma? Are you clear in your mind about how you feel about it? Have you been feeling stressed, nervous? Are you sleeping well? Anything at all that you may want to tell me?"

Usually we don't recognise the point of no return until later but I knew, right then I knew. I could speak up now about the dream, about the horrible feeling in the room at Amy's house and of course about the woods last night. I didn't and that is when I started to lie.

"I think I'm fine actually. Of course it was a big thing, I didn't have any idea what it would be like to shoot someone, but no, I think I'm dealing with it okay." She tilts her head to one side as she studies me.

"Good, that's good. You look a little tired, are you sleeping?"

"Sleeping, oh yeah. I think I've got a bit of a bug coming on and we've all been working hard on this case and I got soaked the other night, didn't I? Well you know how it is."

"Hmm. So, at the moment you don't need any sleeping pills, there's nothing you want to talk about?"

"Sleeping pills, God no. Well, what I mean is no thank you, I've never been one for taking sleeping pills. Thanks though."

"How do you feel about Amy and the obsession that she had with you?"

"Oh, well, yeah it was a bit weird, I admit. Then again it was pretty much what we were trying to do. Well, maybe not quite that, but friendship anyway."

"But it doesn't bother you that she followed you and from what I understand she spied on your home and intended to entice you into a relationship with her?"

"Nope, it's over, isn't it? I guess that's about all you can say."

"And Maria, that case isn't closed is it? Do you feel that the exercise was unsuccessful?"

I mustn't overreact. Take it steady. "Well, I would have preferred to find her, her body of course. You never know, we have an idea now where it could be. Anyway, I'm not sure what's going to happen about all that yet, we have a conference planned for this morning. Actually, I think that, if it's okay I really should be getting back? Are we done, well, you know, have we finished?"

"I think that maybe it would be a good idea if you come back and see me again, maybe a week from now. Sometimes things take a while to settle down, it's possible you could have a reaction later, would you do that?"

"Well I don't think there's any need but I suppose I don't have a lot of choice." Christ, I didn't mean to sound defensive.

She glances down at the paper on the table and then reaches for a blue folder, my file I suppose.

"Okay, you come back again the same time next week and if, in the meantime, you feel you need to talk to me, give me a call." She hands me a business card and then holds out her hand to shake mine.

Closing the door carefully I lean against the cream wall in the corridor. My legs are weak and my hands are quivering. Why, what have I got to hide? She was only trying to help me, why wasn't I honest with her?

Work, that's the answer. Get back to work and keep busy and everything will click back into place.

On top of that, as if it wasn't enough, they have decided to shelve the idea of a search for Maria. Now that we have Amy's confession on the tape that was hidden in my bag, they reckon that it wouldn't serve any purpose. No solid confirmation that the body is in the woods. They must be joking, how can they say that? No money for a prolonged search on the off chance. Of course, if the family cause a fuss there could be a turnaround but as things stand, that's it. How can they do that? How can they leave her there, in the woods? If Amy had killed me would they have left me out there in the dark and the rain? At one time I would have said no way but now, well I just don't know. I argued and tried to force them to alter the decision but, in the end, I could feel that I was losing control. Bill was giving me some funny looks and I had to let it go. For the present time, that's how they couched it – for the present time. She is out there now. Still in that horrible place on her own.

Charlie has come over. I thought I would enjoy the company and he wanted to be with me. Obviously we haven't seen much of each other for ages and he's been patient. Relationships can be so hard when one partner isn't in the Force but he is marvellous. I will make it up to him, let him know that I understand the sacrifices he makes.

It's okay at first, we've had takeaway and some wine and listened to music and it felt normal, ordinary. It's very good.

Of course he assumed he's staying over. Well, so have I. We've had a cuddle on the couch. As I say, normal, and now we have brought our wine with us into the bedroom. He is kind, gentle, he always is. I know he will want all of me tonight. I will give him what he wants. I owe it to him.

He's turned the light out so that there is just the orange glow from the streetlamp and the hall light. I have always liked it like that and he's remembered.

I know it can't be true, I know she can't be here, but the shadow in the corner is Amy, the billow of the curtain in the breeze is Amy, and when I close my eyes and he touches me, it is her hands that I feel. It is her old hands, bony fingers with the knuckles swollen and her skin scratchy and dry.

I try to ride over it, this feeling, but Charlie knows something is wrong and I can't explain it to him. Christ, how do you tell your boyfriend that in the darkness you are making love to a dried-out husk of a woman?

I push him away, the hurt on his face tears at my heart but I can hardly breathe. "It's too early after all the drama. I think you should go, I'm sorry, I'm so sorry." I want him to stay but he is so upset and I feel so bad.

I will spend the night in the chair by the window watching the trees in the churchyard, I can't face the bed.

I need to get this sorted.

I can do it, if I just finish the job and get the enquiry out of the way it'll all be fine, we can be together, we will be happy.

Chapter 34

I'm going to the woods. They have told me not to. First it was Mrs Harker; it was our third appointment. She told me she didn't think I was as well as I imagined. Bill Collins has said that I need to take time off. They don't understand.

Nobody sees, only me. I have to find her. She's out there in the dark on her own. I said I would find her. When we first heard about it all: Amy and the suspicions of her old colleagues to do with Maria's sudden disappearance. Ever since then I was caught up with it. I need to find her and until I do, I can't move on.

I think about Amy and the things that she said, the lies that she told me. There was that night I spent in her house. She crept into my room, she thought I didn't know but oh I knew. All those weeks I spent pretending to be innocent and ignorant and making her believe I wanted to be her friend. It was easy —

the acting and the lying and the pretence – it was easy because it was taking me to Maria.

I can't take it, this lack of closure, so I'm going to the woods and I will find her. *I am coming, Maria.* I will take her away from there and give her peace.

They have made me stay at home. Mrs Harker said I was suffering from PTSD and she has given me a prescription for some stuff to help me to sleep. I don't want to take it but sometimes I need to. Sometimes in the night they are both there, I see them. Amy comes often and she brings Maria to torment me. I won't take the pills tonight, though, because tonight I am going to the woods.

I have to wait until after dark, I can't risk being seen and sometimes Bill calls me during the day. He says he is just checking in but really he is checking up. He is keeping his eye on me. I know he's worried because the enquiry is coming up and I need to be able to give my evidence. I will, I'll tell them all about it. I'll tell them how evil Amy was and then I'll surprise them, I'll tell them that I have found Maria and after that it will be over.

Who would have thought, when we were setting up the cover of Hummingbird, that it would end the way it did? It was all so perfect. It didn't take long for me to get Amy to notice me and then the business with the shawl, oh yes, she fell for it. Because I am similar in looks to poor Maria, we hoped that she would be drawn to me. We hoped that I was a type that would attract her and it worked better than we had hoped. I like to think that I was mostly responsible, made the biggest contribution but now I see. They are all ready to leave it. They've told me the file will still be open, murder cases are never closed but they don't really believe that. They're happy that the guilty have been punished and they think it's enough. They're paying lip service, that's all, a search in due course we're told, once there is more evidence to indicate the location, and loads of other nonsense.

Amy came to me again last night. I know it was a dream. I am not losing my mind. No matter what the psychologist might think, I can tell the difference between reality and imagination. It made me think, though. If she can come to me in a dream then maybe I can go to her. Maybe I can reach her in her own little bit of Hell. If I can reach her, I may be able to communicate and then I can ask her to help me. What difference will it make to her now? She is cursed and will surely spend eternity in purgatory.

I am not sure how to go about it, I have practiced some meditation in a small way in the past but I don't know that it will help now. I'm going to get some books out of the library, things about mind reading, how to heighten your senses, that sort of thing. Nothing too weird. No, not the library – they may be spying on me – I'll buy them. I can go to the Waterstones down near Costa. Hah, what an irony that I should go there where she used to hide to watch me, thinking I didn't know.

I have taken sleeping pills once or twice. At first I didn't want to and then I realised that maybe sleep was a good thing. I dream when I sleep and when I dream, she comes to me. I need to be able to reach her to keep the channels open. I think that maybe I need something stronger than the pills that Mrs Harker gives me. I may need to go and see some of the people down in town in the alleys and the doorways. I will have to be careful though, some of them know me.

Oh Amy, what a tangle we have to sort out. But I can do it, I know I can. I'm strong and I have a purpose, I'm going to find Maria, I have to give her peace.

Chapter 35

It's cold again, and raining. It feels as though it has never stopped for days. The ground is sticky underfoot in places and in others it runs with water, little streamlets gurgling through the undergrowth. I have my torch and my boots. I'm well equipped and I'm not afraid.

The car is well back amongst the trees. It's almost invisible from the road. I would have preferred to drive the great four-wheel drive but it's still impounded. I don't understand why really; everyone knows that Amy was in it and that I was driving. They know that hidden in the back was a hammer and the spade with which she intended to bury my body. Really, what more is there to say about it all? They have to stick to the rules, though, and in truth it was never my car, it was a prop in the pantomime.

I have paced in the darkness and clambered between the trees. Occasionally I believed that I felt near to Maria but it was my desperate imagination and nothing more. I don't know what I am searching for. I don't expect that there is a grave marker, well, not in the usual sense of the word. Maybe Amy placed something there. A stone or a piece of wood to make a sad headstone, I don't know.

I've brought a small spade with me now; it has a folding handle. I am not a fool; I don't expect that I will find her tonight but if I do, I want to be ready. I'll hide this spade because I intend to come back as often as I need to until Maria is away from this place.

I've followed the footpath until I reached the place where she tried to kill me. She had directed me there and I still believe that we were heading for the place where Maria is lying. I think she intended to bury me in the same place. She intended us to be lonely grave companions in the empty wood. I don't know how much further she was taking me but I think that it wouldn't be far. She had taken the hammer from her bag; would she have chosen to kill me there if she was then faced with carrying me a long way? That said, she must have carried Maria, or did she? Did she bring her here and destroy her near to a grave she'd already dug?

I am wet and tired and I need to go home. The car feels cold and the windows have steamed up, so I have to wait for a while until the demister does its work. A wave of exhaustion sweeps through me and I close my eyes for a moment and sink into the silence.

A chill creeps up the back of my neck and the hairs on my arms prickle and tingle. Without moving, I open my eyes. All my senses are alert. Suddenly, I feel alive in a way that I haven't since the night I shot Amy. My eyes swivel to the rear-view mirror. Outside all is darkness. A tiny light is shining in the woods. I can see it like a pinprick of brilliance amongst the trees. A walker? Not on a night like this. Maybe someone looking for a place to dump rubbish. Fly tipping is a continual problem in woodland everywhere but it would have to be a determined fly tipper to come out on a night like this.

As I watch the tiny gleam grows, it wavers back and forth and a little up and down as if someone is walking along the path with a torch. It could be a sightseer – since the incident with the shooting we have had problems with rubbernecks and ghouls. I don't want to leave the spreading warmth of the car but I am a police officer in spite of being signed off for rest, so I have to do my job.

Gently does it, I swing the door as slowly and as quietly as possible. I slide out into the damp coldness. All the time I have to keep the little gleam in sight. It has been still for a while, as if it were waiting for me. I lean back and grab my own torch from the passenger seat. Holding it in front of me but turned off, I take a few steps back in the direction of the trees. The light moves away just a tad, so I pause, I don't want to alarm whoever it is and cause them to run.

I take a couple of steps and the light is still hovering above the path. Another pace or two and it moves away and then stops. I step forward and again. I am nearly at the tree line. The light wavers and flickers as the smaller tree branches move in the slight breeze.

I am at the trees and moving into the deep darkness, I should turn my torch on now and call out but I won't. The light draws me on slowly at the pace that I have set, it travels into the trees. I follow.

Back down the path I've just trodden, on into the gloom, the light travelling just ahead. It pauses at the turn in the path, it waits for me. I am hooked to it, mesmerised. On and on past the awful tree and still on. I am peering into the darkness but I can't see a figure, only the light. It is about the size of a small torch and three feet or so above the ground, glowing white against the darkness of the trees and shrubs. I try to move nearer, pick up the pace a little but I can't gain on it. It's about a hundred yards away, the same distance as when I first saw it. I am certain now, it is for me, I know it is leading me.

We reach a clearing and the light is at the far side. It is a gap in the trees, triangular and almost flat. The ground is covered in tall grasses that are almost black in the night. Around the perimeter there are old trees interspersed with young saplings and there are boulders in the grass, humps and bumps here and there. The light is in the shrubs at the other side of the space. It is stationary now and I still don't know what it is. I can't see a figure; I haven't been able to make out who is carrying it. I move onto the flatter ground and as I do the light falls to the ground and is extinguished. I am left in the darkness. For a moment it is complete and then my night vision kicks in and I can make out the clearing again, grey and greyer, deeps and shadows and black trees opposite me. The night is silent and I know, suddenly I know with a total certainty that she is here. Maria has found me and brought me here. This is where she has been buried.

Chapter 36

I couldn't dig. Stupid, stupid. I had taken the spade back to the car after all and then when I tried to retrace my steps I turned around in the gloom and spent an age floundering back and forth taking wrong paths and turnings. I wasn't afraid, I knew she was there waiting for me. I had to leave her, though; yet again I let her down.

I can't ask for help; I mustn't mention this. Bill would listen to me with a patient expression as I told him of my trip to the woods, the light, the clearing and on and on. Then he would shake his head and sigh, I can hear the sigh, and then he would refer me to Mrs Harker who would tell me that I shouldn't be visiting the woods. It would be such a help, though, to look through the files, see the plans of the woodland and get some bearings.

I know that the other way would be to go back on my own with a long stick and work my way around the clearing. I would poke the stick into the soft earth and then smell the end. If I found the grave the smell of putrefaction and decay would reward my search. I can't do it. I can't risk disturbing Maria in such a way; the thought appals me. I will not poke and prod at her sleeping body.

The dawn finds me sleepless, lying on my bed partly dressed, staring into the dimness as I have through the long night. I clamber from the bed as the day creeps through the gap in the curtains. A hot shower eases my aching muscles but does little for my aching head.

I have made a decision of sorts to go to Amy's house. There may be something there that can help me. Perhaps she made a record of some sort, a plan, a note in a diary. Something. Surely being responsible for the death of another person who she believed she loved she recorded it somewhere. How well I know that such violence plays with your brain. It nibbles at your consciousness and pricks at your subconscious. It never lets you forget, not for a moment. She must have recorded something, surely.

The road is deserted at this time of the day in a million other neighbourhoods like this. Am I the only one to feel that there is no other neighbourhood like this? I have walked to keep myself as discreet as possible. The little gate swings open easily and I follow the concrete path round to the back of the house. The little patio looks forlorn, it hasn't been long but this garden knows it is abandoned. It will be a long time now before anyone will pay it any attention.

The window frames are old and some are a little warped. The security is practically non-existent. It only requires a quick bang against the kitchen window. If you know where to direct the force, these windows are easy to open.

It is a bit too high for me to reach but the patio chairs are conveniently to hand. When I drag one across the boards it carves a trail of clean wood on the mossy surface and the wood on the chair arm is damp and spongy. It holds my weight though and I can lean through the window and turn the key in the lock. If I was still working on this case, I would have someone on the carpet for leaving the key in the lock. It is such a careless thing to do but it has played into my hands beautifully. There is a lock at the top of the door and for a while I am juggling with a metal stake before it slides back. There we are, the door is unlocked, and I tread gently into the kitchen.

Inside smells of disuse and decay. Someone will have to empty the cupboards here and the fridge. It could be a long time before anyone comes back to care for this place and all of the beauty will be spoiled by then. It would be better for it to be knocked down. That's not my concern at the moment.

I pass through to the hall on my way to her study. How familiar it all is, there isn't much disturbance. A few papers are discarded on a chair and the drawers of the desk are open and have been emptied. There is a strong stale smell coming from the vases of flowers which have died and tainted the water.

I search for her diary but find nothing. From the dearth of documentation, I assume that a lot of her records have been taken away. If they're in the office at the police station they're beyond my reach.

In the lounge are more dead flowers, more stinking water and the place has a fine covering of dust. How she would hate this. Amy, so house-proud, finicky even.

I flop onto the settee and lay my head back against the cushions. It feels cold and it's smelly and unpleasant and I shouldn't be here. My eyes are heavy, it's hard to keep them open. It's an age since I had any real sleep, I sink into the darkness and let it claim me.

Chapter 37

I stretch my legs under the warmth of the duvet and poke at my pillow. Without really emerging from sleep my mind registers a strangeness. Where's my other pillow? On the floor or pushed up against the headboard? I fumble above my head, still lost in my sleepy fug. No, it's not there. On the floor then. With a sigh and a lazy shuffle, I trail an arm over the edge of the bed and search with my fingertips. Damn, still no pillow.

On the verge of turning and leaning out of bed to find it, my senses climb to another level. I hold my breath as my body freezes. This isn't my bed, no need to open my eyes, this just isn't my space. Above that knowledge lays another even more frightening, I'm not alone. A thrill of fear trickles along my arms and down my back. I open my eyes a tiny slit and roll my eyeballs sideways. Where the hell is this?

Some sense of self-preservation has overtaken me and kept me immobile as I force my thoughts back to the last memory. I was in Amy's house and I had plonked down on the settee for a moment. That's the last thing that I remember. Is this another blackout like the one that landed me in the woods? If it is, where has my unconscious self taken me now?

I hear breathing. I peer through the dim light. A tall figure is outlined in the light from the partly opened doorway.

"Christ." I jar my neck shooting upwards in the bed. Amy has moved into my room from the landing.

"Hush now, it's okay, don't be afraid. I heard you cry out in your sleep and came to make sure that you were alright."

"Amy, no that's not you. Amy."

"Of course it's me, why who else would it be? Are you alright? Were you dreaming? Shall I bring you a drink? Water, warm milk?"

My hand is scrabbling desperately at my side for the lamp on the bedside table. "Amy, you're dead, it's not you. What the hell is this? Shit, where's the light?"

"My goodness, Hannah, you have had a nasty dream. I'm sorry, my dear, I forgot to plug in the light, here, let me turn the room light on for you."

"No!" I didn't want to see her; she can't be here. This is a dream; it has to be a dream. I fling myself from the bed. This is Amy's house, the room that she had prepared for me. My perfume on the dressing table and a cream shawl just like mine laid on the end of the bed. I look down, I am fully dressed, I even have my shoes on. What the hell am I doing in bed with my shoes on?

My eyes are adjusted now to the dimness enabling me to peer at the figure in the doorway. She stands with a hand stretched towards the light switch, her face turned sideways towards me. It is Amy. Cold, clammy sweat makes me shiver as I try to make sense of what's happening. I take one terrified step towards her. It's Amy, there's no doubt. She's dressed in the clothes that she was wearing when we went to the woods to find Maria's grave.

I can't speak, it's impossible to make sense of this. We're a tableau, a still life for several moments as my mind spins and roars with fear and bewilderment, and yes, with hope. Could it be that I'd dreamed it all, could it be that we hadn't gone to the woods and I didn't shoot her after all? As the thought takes hold, my subconscious self grasps at it. Is this a second chance? I step forward reaching my hand towards her. She moves towards me, she is limping.

As she moves across the carpet towards me, the light from the doorway increases and gleams on the sticky mess that has formed around her feet. She trails the darkness after her, it seeps from the top of her leg and slithers down to her foot where it pools around her feet as she makes her stumbling way across the room.

Am I dreaming now, had I dreamt before? She holds out her arms. "Hannah, my dear. You must come with me now. I must have you, surely you know that. You will be mine; it is destiny. Come with me now, don't struggle any more. We can go together; I will help you." She has reached me and she touches my face with frozen fingers that are slick with blood. I scream, I hear myself scream. I hear the screeching spiralling upwards as a great dark cloud descends and blessed oblivion takes me away.

Chapter 38

I'm cold and cramped. One leg is twisted under my body and has lost all feeling. I'm slumped on the floor at the foot of the bed in the dark. The smell and the cold and the horrible emptiness overwhelm me. I push to my feet and stagger stiffly for the stairs.

I have no idea how long I've been unconscious in the horrible bedroom but it must have been a while to leave me so shivery and out of sorts. As I clatter down the stairs and across the hall, I struggle to push back the memory, the awful, terrible memory of Amy standing in the doorway bleeding onto the carpet and then dragging her wounded self towards me. I can still feel the imprint of her cold, dead fingers on my face. I scrub at my cheek to obliterate the phantom feeling.

I try to blank it. What happened? I cannot, will not, face it. She seemed to have been there but I know it's not possible. I heard her speak, I felt her touch me.

I throw open the door and fall into the real world. Slamming the wood back into the frame I hear the Yale lock click into place. Down the narrow pathway and off down the street still struggling against the pictures that want to show themselves to my waking self.

I could go tomorrow and see Mrs Harker, for sure I need help. Wait, what can I say, how can I explain it? I know they're already worried about me; they think that I can't cope, think that I am losing my grip. If I tell them that I've been at the house, that I was searching for answers then they'll definitely sign me off longer from work and it will show on my record. I have worked hard to get where I am, I am not giving it all up for the sake of my imagination; that's all this is, imagination.

I have to admit that I haven't been able to cope with this as well as I would have hoped. When I first went undercover and we set up the Hummingbird offices and the whole plan to attract her and to trap her, I was really keen, excited. I thought it would be a breeze. Well, it wasn't as if she were some sort of drug cartel or terrorist cell. One woman, one woman who we all believed was a murderer, but one woman none the less.

It was the shooting that threw me. I had never understood what that would be like. The blood and the sight of her lying on the ground shaking, and knowing that I had done that. No matter what else happens with my life, no matter even how this turns out, I did that. I need to get to grips with it, to face it and to put it in perspective and then all will be fine.

I don't believe in spirits, hauntings, premonitions – it's rubbish. No, I don't need to see anyone about this, I'll just sort it myself.

My flat welcomes me like an old friend. She has never been here; her presence hasn't tainted this atmosphere. I take a shower, a big whisky and wrap myself in the comfort of my duvet. Tomorrow I will start to come back from this, tomorrow I will put her behind me.

Chapter 39

"So, are you okay to do this, Hannah?"

"Yeah, 'course I am. I told you, Sarge. I'm absolutely fine. I don't know why I'm not at work. Anyway, I'll be glad to get this out of the way. Once the enquiry is over, we can move on, can't we?"

"Well, we have to be guided by the psychologist and she thinks that you need more time. To be honest you do look bloody awful. I know you said you'd been sleeping but I don't believe you, you've got bags under your eyes and you just don't look good."

"Aw thanks, that's just what I want to hear." I try to laugh but it's hollow and only serves to increase the worried expression on Bill's face. I resist the temptation to pace back and forth in the grey corridor but the effort to hold my hands still in my lap and to sit quietly on the chair is immense.

The shooting was righteous, I know it was. My life was at risk, I had no choice. The general feeling in the office is that this will be a quick formality, all the evidence has been examined and nobody can find any reason for me to worry. They have all dropped little notes into the mail – support and encouragement and kindness. Still, I am tormented and anxious.

I am tormented by my failure. I know we're all supposed to be in a team, no individuals, all for one and blah blah but it seems that I'm the only one who feels that we've failed. I have left Maria, she is still alone in an unmarked, lonely grave and I'm dreadfully saddened whenever I think of her. I've told myself there is no more to be done, it's over. We know now for certain that she's dead. Her family have been informed and by all accounts have begun to grieve and accept.

I never even met her, I didn't know her and yet she has my life in a stranglehold. I need, desperately, to find her and to lay her to rest with the dignity and recognition that she deserves.

At the start of the whole thing she was just a name on a piece of paper. Even after I met Amy and the whole thing had fallen into place so beautifully, she was simply the reason behind it. I can't say when it changed but at some time during the weeks that we followed her murderer and in the final days and in those dreadful last hours I became so very close to her.

When I knew that Amy had fallen completely for the plan and that even more than that she had become infatuated with me, the way that she had with

Maria, then I felt our lives intertwining. I could have been her. She had died at the hands of a twisted and disturbed woman and I could have met the same fate but for the grace of whatever kindness watched over me in the dark woods.

On top of all of that is Amy. She watches me. I feel her near me constantly. I should talk to Mrs Harker about it but I'm afraid to. She won't understand, I don't understand and I am very afraid because I don't know what to do.

Bill's right, I'm not sleeping. I'm afraid to close my eyes because whenever I do, I risk her coming through to me. She wants me I know that she is still waiting for me. I sound mad, I know I sound mad and I don't know what to do.

Chapter 40

The enquiry is behind me. It was as everyone imagined and I was exonerated. The board accepted that I had no choice and I acted in self-defence. There will be a coroner's inquest about the death of Maria. Now that we have the statements made by Amy and we're sure that Maria is dead then the formalities can go ahead. I must put it away. I have to accept that I'll probably never find her.

I am so very tired. Sleep is an unreachable luxury. Each night I close my eyes and slide into the tantalising drift and the nightmare starts. I see the woods, the clearing and the humps and bumps in the earth. Usually to preserve my sanity, my instincts for self-preservation pitch in and suddenly I'm sitting bolt upright. As the nerve endings in my arms and legs tingle and hum, my heart pounds with fear. I haven't bothered with the bedroom for a couple of weeks now.

I have a duvet on the couch in the living room. I read or watch the television until my eyes are closing. I drag the cover over me and let my head fall back. Soothing darkness envelops me, my muscles start to unwind and warm and I drift. As I reach this stage the dream begins.

In the dream the wind howls in the treetops, the moonlit clouds scud in the silver grey of the night sky and great black branches reach and bend towards me. It's always the same. Each time I fall a little deeper and stay longer, before my brain forces me back home.

I'm alone in the clearing in the stormy night, the leaves and grasses are darkened and monotone. Standing in the centre of the grassy area I spin slowly, my eyes raking the undergrowth. Round and round peering into the gloom searching for the grave.

Last night my dream self stepped forward two paces. The grass under my feet moved as the ground heaved and bucked. The leaves dripped and shone with moisture. White roots gleamed and the trees leaned and toppled with a great sucking sound. The sods turned back as the ground opened to reveal a great chasm. The darkness in the grave was complete, a rich blackness, and there in a muddy pool at the bottom was a body. It was naked, I could see rags of clothes and the gleam of bones shining through but the eyes were real and open and glinting with moonlight. The body was skeletal but the face was whole and the face was mine, then Maria – the same as the photographs I have seen of her – then Amy, and then me. It was a ghastly, ever-changing, shifting triumvirate.

As I watched, the fingers moved and the arms lifted and stretched towards me, beckoning, willing me down into the darkness. I leaned further over the hole stretching my hands towards the dead thing trying to bring it up, to rescue it. My own face stared up at me as I listened to the footsteps creeping across the grass and swishing nearer and nearer. I was frozen in fear, I couldn't turn even though the threat was nearer with every second. The face in the grave changed. It was Maria, it was me, now Maria. A hand grabbed my shoulder and spun me to face Amy standing amongst the fallen branches and the uprooted trees with the great hammer raised as it was the moment I pulled the trigger.

I am terrified of tonight. I dread closing my eyes. I have drunk coffee and brandy and taken pills to keep me awake. I want to sleep; I desperately need to sleep but I don't dare.

Chapter 41

I am wired and strung out, the coffee and the pills have me buzzing with tension, my head is spinning. I'm exhausted and exhilarated all at once. The room is melting in front of my face and the walls warp and bend as I watch them. There's buzzing in my ears, deep inside, and I can feel my heart pounding in my chest and through my veins, thundering at the back of my head and pulsing in my eyeballs.

I don't know what the pills were. I bought them from a low life down in the alley by the park. I won't sleep, I know that, I won't ever sleep again. I don't need to; I can go on like this forever.

I have waited long enough now for them to help me, my so-called colleagues, my friends. I thought that I would be going back to work when the enquiry was over. That was to be my chance to make them listen to me. We could have gone with the dogs and the heat seekers and the whole bloody lot and we could have found her in one day and then it would have been over. Instead of that I am still stuck here at home in this damn flat. They won't even let me near the office anymore. They are talking about more doctors, more drugs, hospital even. Can't they see that all I need is to find her? My sister in torment, my other half, Maria.

I must set her free, she must find peace and then I can rest. She needs to know that we understand. She needs to know that we didn't forget about her. The only way to show her is to bring her back from that horrible deadly place. She deserves that from us, surely.

I'm going to go to the woods myself. I'll dig up that whole bloody clearing and I'll find her myself. I can do it on my own if they won't listen. If they won't help, fine, I don't need them. They've never understood, none of them. The blasted psychologist; Sergeant Collins – my best mate, isn't he? Oh yes, Bill my mate, but what good has he been to us?

I have to get her out of there and I have to do it soon. Amy won't leave me alone until I finish this. I haven't told anyone about Amy, ha, imagine how they'd react to that. Only I know. I haven't told them about the visits. In the dark when the terrors have made me sleepless and the memories nibble at the back of my brain. She comes then when I'm weak and when I'm alone. I am so alone.

Right, I've got my shovel, a nice long shovel this time – it's in the back of the car – and a blanket for poor Maria. That poor victim left in the woods forgotten, ignored and discounted. I'll bring her back, Amy can't have her, she didn't get me and now I'm going to take Maria away from her and then she'll leave me alone…

The woods are dark, hah, of course they are, stupid, stupid. Down here, down this path back behind the little gate and towards the hillocks. I know the way now with my eyes closed. Watch me, see, I'm walking with my eyes closed. Ooops, shit, now I'm in the mud. No matter, I'm nearly there.

Here, here it is the clearing. It's my dream of course but I'm in charge now. I'm awake and I'm strong, I am so strong and powerful. Listen everybody, listen to me. "I'M STRONG. I'M GOING TO FIND HER." No, no, mustn't do that, mustn't shout. I look like a mad person. I just need to be calm and sensible. I need to think.

I'll start by the big oak. If I was burying a body I'd put it there, wouldn't I? Ah but wait, look, look there, a willow, a big willow. That's where she is, that's where Amy with her arty farty ways and her poncey music and her posh house would put her. Underneath the willow.

The soil is soft here, muddy a bit but quite soft and I can shift it easily, I think. The bloody roots are in the way but that's good because if they're in my way they must have been in Amy's as well – ha ha, see. Now this spot here, where there's a gap between the roots…

It's taking a long time; the rain has started again and the walls of this hole keep collapsing and I have to clear the same mud that I've just dug before I can make any progress. It won't stop me, though. I'm going to do it. My only worry is that I won't have time, it's after midnight already. What time does it get light? How long have I got?

The hole is big now, I can stand in it. If only it didn't keep falling back in on itself, I would have finished by now. The rain is heavier. See, if they had listened, we would have had a tent over this and more hands. Why am I having to do this on my own?

I was right, there she is. I see her. Oh poor, poor thing. Not even a coffin just a piece of blanket or something and all the soil down on her face and in her hair. I'm standing with my feet either side of where she's lying, they slip and slide with the collapse of the walls. I need to get nearer. I'll scrape away at the soil gently, setting her free. I need to use my hands, though, the spade is too big and I have to be so careful. Poor fragile thing, she has spent so long waiting for me.

"I'm here now, Maria, I won't leave you".

I wish this mud wasn't clinging to my hands, it runs back down my arms when I try to lob it over the top of the hole. This is so difficult. I shouldn't have to do this on my own.

Aw no, her hair is tangled around my fingers, it's wet and it comes away in great clinging, winding clumps. I'm so sorry, Maria, I'm trying not to hurt you, I really am.

It's me and it's Maria together in the dark earth and now here Amy comes, I feel her. She's near, the air hums now with the evil she brings. I'll hide, I won't let her find me, find us. Down in the dark, down beside Maria.

It's soft and dark down here and the water is running in little rivulets through the walls. I feel calm though, here down in the earth, it's quiet and dark and soft. The bottom is flooding but I'm not cold anymore, the shivering has stopped. I don't know if I'll be able to lift her out, though. I'll wait until Amy has gone. I'll sense it and then I can get us out. The walls are slipping down and the mud is falling on Maria. I need to stop and think, I need to take stock now and work out what to do. I need to protect her from the rain and the falling sides of the grave. I'll just sit down here beside her and hold her to me. I can pull her over here in the blanket. I'll wrap her in my arms and protect us from the falling soil while I take stock. I'll wait until Amy's gone and then I'll work out what to do next. If the walls hold.

The space is getting smaller, I'm trying hard not to disturb Maria, she's too fragile, her bones move and separate. I'm sorry. The water is rising quickly in the bottom now and mud is cascading in clods from the walls and the edge at the top. I think I should try and get out.

I don't want to leave her, but I know where she is. I can bring them back; make them bring a coffin and a shroud. Bill will listen to me now.

I'll climb out.

The walls are running with the flood. If I can get a grip, I'll be fine. I need to push my fingers into the mud. Sludge is pulling me down into the darkness. The walls are bulging inwards, little rivers gushing through.

Won't somebody come? Will nobody help us?

Chapter 42

I have lost her; the water has reached above my thighs. I can't see her anymore. I don't want to stand on her, I can't bear the thought of her body under my feet. The small bones, her fingers and her toes had fallen away and the mud swallowed them. It is hideous down here and I'm afraid. There's a roaring in my head and my eyes are stinging with grit and water.

Now, there is a light, it is blinding, sudden and searing. The shock sends me onto my back, into the mud and bones, I swallow foul liquid.

"Bloody hellfire, Hannah, keep still or you'll have the whole thing in on top of you!"

"Sarge, Sarge – is that you?"

"Of course it's me, you daft sod. Christ the whole thing is going, give me your hand."

I reach and stretch but it's too far and too wet. I see him turn away. "Don't, don't leave me."

"Hey, one of you sods, hold my legs." Now he lies on the floor.

"Bill, don't, you'll fall in."

"Shut up and give me your bloody hand."

I reach and reach again, the grave pulls me back, my feet suck and sink deeper.

Now he has me, his fingers touch mine, they slip, we reach again. He grabs my wrist and pulls, my shoulders scream, "No, no don't, my legs are stuck." More hands reach for me, they grab my arms, dragging me away from where she lies. One last, huge pull and they have me free. Clods of earth cascade and cover her as she gives me up.

His coat is warm around my shoulders, it's ruined of course, "You'll never get the mud out of this, sir."

He shakes his head, his eyes gleam with moisture.

"How did you find me?"

"The patrol saw your car. They'd logged it here before and so this time they ran the plates. Bloody pool car so they checked in to see what was going down. It's logged to us so it came through to me. You shouldn't have had the bloody car anyway, you were supposed to be signed off."

"You saved me."

"Yes, I bloody did and you owe me." His arms around my shoulders pull me closer as the flash of blue sparks in the trees.

"Come on, let's get you into that ambulance. Let's get you well again, eh?"

"Yes please." He helps me to my feet and we turn together to the half-filled hollow. "I found her though, didn't I? I found Maria."

"Yes, Hannah. It seems you did."

The End

If you enjoyed this book, please let others know by leaving a quick review on Amazon. Also, if you spot anything untoward in the paperback, get in touch. We strive for the best quality and appreciate reader feedback.

editor@thebookfolks.com

www.thebookfolks.com

Other books by Diane Dickson

The DI Tanya Miller series:

BRAZEN ESCAPE
BRUTAL PURSUIT
BURNING GREED
BROKEN ANGEL
BLURRED LINES

The DI Jordan Carr series:

BODY ON THE SHORE
BODY BY THE DOCKS
BODY OUT OF PLACE
BODY IN THE SQUAT
BODY IN THE CANAL
BODY ON THE ESTATE
BODY BELOW THE BRIDGE
BODY IN THE WAY

Others:

HOPELESS
TWIST OF TRUTH
TANGLED TRUTH
BONE BABY
LEAVING GEORGE
PICTURES OF YOU
LAYERS OF LIES
DEPTHS OF DECEPTION
YOU'RE DEAD
SINGLE TO EDINBURGH
THE GRAVE

www.ingramcontent.com/pod-product-compliance
Lightning Source LLC
Chambersburg PA
CBHW031000210726
48290CB00007B/2394